MW01714839

The Greys

by

Becky Barnard and Dave Housley

pandamoon publishing

www.pandamoonpublishing.com

Art Direction by Don Kramer: Pandamoon Publishing
Illustrations by Don Kramer and Pauline Dimla: Pandamoon Publishing
Editing by Zara Kramer, Forrest Driskel, Kathleen Bosman, and Rachel Schoenbauer: Pandamoon Publishing

Library of Congress Cataloging-in-Publication Data is on file at the Library of Congress, Washington, DC

Edition: 1, version. 1.00

ISBN-13: 978-1-950627-48-6

Dedication

To all the good weirdos. Keep it weird.

For the Moises, some of the best good weirdos.

Becky Bernard

The Greys

Prologue: Eunice

The invasion has started, but the agent is opting out. She stands on top of the hill and watches the field team deploy. Tries to etch every face—human and not—into her brain. She'll need to remember them later.

Will she even be around to remember? If not, her replacement will need to know. There's always a replacement. It is protocol. She pulls a cell phone out of her bag, disables the flash, and takes photos. Click. The barn. Zoom in on the fire licking up the exterior wall. Purple flames? Purple flames. Potassium chloride burns purple. This batch of eggs must have needed more salt. Click. Field agents from multiple planets taking measurements. Click. A number of delegates, arguing about policy. Click.

The member planets of the Council are evenly represented, but that's not a surprise. As soon as the current crisis is managed, each terranaut team will report back to their own planets. What happened, who was to blame, and why, of course, it wasn't them.

The wind shifts, bathing her in the heat of the purple flames. She can feel the sweat matting her hair down on the back of her neck. One more layer to tolerate. She whorls the hair up on her head and secures it with the ever-present hair tie on her wrist. The elastic isn't part of the standard uniform, and the hair is longer than regulation. She likes it longer—more flattering for her face. Silly for them to not mesh the regulation facial features with the regulation hairstyle. A small thing, too small to note in her nightly paperwork, but maybe symbolic of the overall problems with the mission. Ignoring the small details on the ground that would have made them more successful, handing down orders from a million miles away.

Management has so many orders.

The agent uploads the photos to a private Instagram account. The account has two followers and only posts occasionally. *Keep it simple.* Her followers will see the new photo notification and enact their own version of protocol. Management won't like it. But by the time Management finds out, the agent won't care.

She slides off her backpack and loops her shoulders in little circles, wincing as they pop-crunch. Stiff muscles? Bad connection between the biosuit and her actual body? Or is her body starting to break down? Too many early mornings following her own leads instead of Management's? Too busy to build herself back up? It's hard to tell.

She would love to take the Euniform off one last time. Leave it draped on a rotting log like a snakeskin. Feel the sun, the moon, and stars on grey skin instead of whatever this Earth tone is. At least one tiny ray of starlight would be from the Cygnus galaxy. From home.

The upload progress bar creeps from ten to twenty to fifty percent. She watches the action down on the farm. Two delegates are rehearsing their lines—they'll pretend to be the family that owns the farm. They give each other pointers on the accent. Indiana. Not quite flat Midwestern, not quite Southern drawl, not quite Mid-Atlantic. Again, unremarkable.

They exchange variations on "just so glad we're safe" and "we'll probably stay with my sister in Wisconsin for a bit" as they swipe through life-sized holograms of themselves in different outfits. Overalls? Too cliché. Silk boxers and a tiny, red nightgown? Too sexy and therefore too memorable. Sweatpants and hoodies from Danaville High, rumpled as if pulled out of a hamper and put on in a hurry? Perfect. The delegates grab the holograms out of the air and fling them on their own bodies. Their forms blur momentarily, and when they come back into focus, they're in the sweats.

The scientists finish their measurements, and the cleanup team moves in. A few flamethrowers come out of a windowless van. The agent can hear the whoosh up on the hill, smell the burning corn husks as ordinary orange-red flames engulf the field.

She smiles. It smells like the day she followed the directions on the popcorn bag, cooking it for the prescribed five minutes and scorching it black. They ran the bag out into the backyard, dumped it in the fire ring, laughed, and watched it smoke. "Eunie, you can't follow protocol all the time. Sometimes you just have to trust your gut. Wing it once in a while."

Well, Eunice is winging it now. She checks the phone. *Upload successful. Good.* And a notification of her own. "@KLA is now following you: [Confirm] [Deny]" And a direct message: "Take me with U."

Damn. She really is smart. Maybe too smart. But that's why Eunice can't follow protocol this time, has to find her own way. Too many of them are too smart. Too many that are kind and fun and interesting. She cannot confirm the request—some secrets have to stay secret, for everyone's safety—but she can't ignore it either.

She crouches down and draws a smiley face in the dirt. She takes a photo and pulls up @KLA's phone number. One last text. The last of thousands. It's such a shame this friendship has to end.

Suddenly, a subsonic acoustic wave swells through her body, turning her guts into ice and setting her hearts racing. One of the other terranauts is shouting in their native frequency instead of using his Earth voice box—panic overriding protocol. She looks at the barn, and she knows that this is the last time it will seem this peaceful, a landscape painting that's about to burst into a million pieces. She sees the ground crew racing away.

The barn explodes, but she never hears it. The shock wave rolls across the field, flattening the rest of the corn and ripping apart the few cattle on the farm. The force reaches Eunice's hilltop seconds before the sound.

In the end, all that remains of Agent Eunice Tiffany is a single tooth.

Chapter 1
Six Earth Months Later

"Come on, Deerdra," Father says, tapping his fingers on the steering wheel. "We are going to being tardy!" A pause. "Late for arrival? Tardy? Is correct?"

"Yes," I reply. "Late. Tardy. Not on time. Just…just give me one more minute."

We are in a parking lot a few blocks away from my new high school. I angle the visor mirror, trying to see my face and outfit.

This top. I do not think I like this top. Colonel Muckinzee recommended I dress like the teenagers in the Sunday newspaper advertisements. There was a girl with dark hair like the hair they have given me, freckles like they have given me, a girl who was approximately my dimensions. She was wearing this top. But that girl looked like she would step off the page and blend into any high school in America. No worries about startling the crowd, causing them to stampede or whatever it is that scared humans do. Even with her above-average facial symmetry and brand-new wardrobe, she was just a slightly more attractive member of the herd.

My makeup is satisfactory—"neutral natural" palette, precision-applied to my biosuit while I was in the regeneration chamber last night. My hair, though, is all wrong. I pull at the bang—is that what they call it, the bang? That can't be right. Why would they call the parts of your hair that hang down over your eyes the same thing as the retort of a deadly weapon? Why would they let their hair hang down over their eyes in the first place? Like so much of what they do on this planet, it just doesn't make any sense. No sense at all. And they don't blend with the complicated braid that my mother designed for me this morning. I adjust the mirror and try to smooth the bangs back into the twists and knots.

"Thirty seconds, Deerdra," says Father. "As your mission commander, I must insist."

"Father, you don't understand how important this is. They say I will only have one chance to make a first impression, and these czubastic bangs…I need the humans to accept me. To befriend me."

"This is not Indiana's Next Top Best Friend, and I haven't seen anything in their protocol excusing tardiness due to bad bangs, Deerdra. Efficiency is a top priority here."

"Fine. Then I will obey protocol." I slide my hand to the nape of my neck, find the small seam, and fold the hairpiece up and forward a few inches, like flipping a swim cap inside-out, just enough to see the braids in the mirror. I tuck and twist the rest of the bangs into the pattern.

"AGENT GREY!" barks Father.

I snap into a salute, leaving the flap on my biosuit open. I can feel the car's cool air blowing on my skin. My actual skin.

"Commander," I reply, looking straight forward. "Protocol dictates I stay within my biosuit at all times, minus three conditions: extreme duress, time spent in a regeneration chamber, or extraction protocol initiation."

My mouth goes dry. I feel like I've swallowed a golf ball. "We…we are technically in a regeneration chamber. The car has that capability." Now I'm blinking but too fast. Why am I blinking so fast? Has my biosuit malfunctioned already? "And…Commander? Father? I am about to start my first day of high school. My first day of ANY school. It's my mission to blend in and make friends, and I can't even get this stupid hair right."

"Deerdra." Father gently reseals the nape of my neck, then puts his palm on my head and kneads, just like he used to when I was a little girl. "I know this is hard," he says. "We are asking a lot of you. The Council is asking a lot of all of us."

Father hesitates, and I glance at him in the rearview mirror. His biosuit was designed to be slightly below average. Neither small nor large. Hair thinning but not yet balding. Worry lines at the corners of his eyes that would come with a demanding-but-boring desk job and a bright-but-not-exceptional teenager.

He looks at the ceiling like he's trying to see through the car and the ridiculous blue sky, through their moon and solar system and all of the many galaxies we passed through on our journey here, like he is trying to see all the way to Anthea. He sighs. "What we're doing here, it's important," he says.

"Important? We're just doing research. Same as all the missions before us."

"There's something you should know," he says. I can hear him vacillating between being my father and my Mission Leader. "We are…rooting for you. We are all rooting for you."

"I don't understand."

"Home is…" He takes a deep breath. "Our planet. Anthea. It is dying." He opens his mouth to say more but then just lets that word sit there between us. He rubs the back of his own neck, fingers playing at the invisible seam in his own biosuit.

"Dying?" I say.

"Do you remember," he says, "when you were very little and we could go outside without protective coating on your sarisuit? Or when sarisuits did not have respirators?"

"Dying?" I say. All of a sudden, all the whispers, all the allusions to the importance of our mission make sense.

"We're here for many reasons," he says. "Including evaluation. Earth is one of the finalists."

"Evaluation?" I start. Then I, too, look up. I have only seen Anthean blue skies in the library. Ancient history, to be specific. "Oh," I say.

"Yes," he says. He almost puts his hand back on my forehead, but instead smooths my hairpiece once more, runs his finger—"William Grey's" stubby, putty-colored human finger, not my Father's elegant steel-toned digits—along the neck seam to double-check the seal. He nods his head once in crisp approval, trying to move back from Father to Commander. "But there is still time. In the meantime," he says, "focus on the mission. My mission, me and your mother, our mission is evaluation. To see if this could be our home. Your mission is to find out what happened to your predecessor, the lost hero Eunice Tiffany. Today, that means school. You cannot be tardy."

I take a deep breath. Balance the biosuit. Focus on the mission.

My name is Deerdra Grey. Here on Earth, I am seventeen years old. I am going to find Eunice Tiffany and save my world.

Chapter 2
Not Like You or Me

We pull up to a red brick building. The sign in front reads DANAVILLE SENIOR HIGH—FIGHT, FOXES, FIGHT. Father comes to a lurching stop. He had to drive two miles an hour over the posted limit to get me to school on time, and this breach of protocol has him flustered.

Herds of human teenagers hurry toward the school. The behavioral models are correct: the students are bunched together in small groups, talking and laughing. Many are on wheels: cars, bicycles, the low-slung street-riding devices known as skateboards. If they are so unhappy with their feet and legs, I wonder, why don't they change them?

"Deerdra," Father says, shifting into Mission Leader mode again. "These people. Humans. There's something you need to understand. They are not like you or me. They are not like us. They are not…advanced. They have only traveled to their moon. Their moon! This is an entire planet, an entire race, and they have not made it past their very own moon. Do you see what I am saying?"

"I…" Suddenly there's a clatter outside, a burst of laughter and shouts. I turn to see a group of girls approaching. It's my first time seeing them in real life, but there they're just as terrifying and spectacular as they had appeared in the classification charts: Popular Girls. They are led by a tall one with yellow hair: the Alpha Popular.

"I need to explain this to you, Deerdra," Father says, but I wave him off. The Populars approach a girl with dark clothing and bright red lipstick, sitting off to the side with headphones in her ears. A tall, dark-haired Popular approaches while the lead stays behind. Pack hunters. The pursuing Popular makes a show of reading something aloud off of her phone, but I can't hear what. The group bursts into laughter. Several boys approach. Jocks, perhaps? They make such a production about laughing that I know that whatever was said to the Unpopular wasn't actually funny.

The Unpopular just extends her central finger, pushes at her earbuds, and walks away. Somehow, some of the power in this interaction shifts back to her. Her shoulders are straight, and she doesn't look back.

Her reaction goes against everything I've been taught about conflict resolution, yet I am feeling…admiration? Curiosity?

The dark-haired Popular's jaw clenches, and she looks back at the Alpha Popular. The Alpha missed the entire scene. Instead, she's moving her phone around, checking her hair, and trying to get the perfect angle for a selfie.

"Deerdra!" Father says. "This is important. Remember that these…people…are not your equals. The difference between us and them is the difference between them and their cows."

"They eat cows, Father."

He nods from side to side the way he does when he's thinking. "We will not eat them, of course."

I look out at the schoolyard, and a wave of an unpleasant sensation floods my system.

"Father? I think there's something wrong with my biosuit? I feel like my body wants to run even though the danger assessment is low."

"That's good, Deerdra. It means the sympathetic nervous system simulation is working. It will give you a better frame of reference for human emotions. Reactivate your parasympathetic nervous protocol, and it will balance out."

"How?"

"Breathe. Slowly, using your abdominal muscles."

I inhale and exhale a few times. New biochemicals wash through my circulatory system and cancel the nervous feeling. Mostly. My hands and feet still tingle, but it's manageable.

"You will optimize this, Deerdra. You exceeded expectations on every practice scenario, you have reviewed decades of Earth media, and I am arrogant of you."

"You are proud of me," I say reflexively.

Father smiles and kneads my forehead briefly. Too fast for it to draw suspicion from outside our vehicle but enough to quell the nervous sensation nearly completely. For a moment, I'm home again. And then, always the Mission Leader, he pretends to straighten my collar and rechecks the seam at the nape of my neck. Can't let them see who I really am. Not today. Not ever. *Fit in.*

"Yes. I am proud of you."

I place my hand on the door handle and pull.

Chapter 3
I Am New

I push through the doors and am enveloped in chaos—laughing and talking and hugging, students moving from one place to another or clumped into groups. The building smells of people and sweat and chlorine and food and perfume and a thousand other organic and inorganic things. I can't move. I'm drowning in sensory sludge.

I rub my palm with my thumb, lowering the sensitivity of my biosuit. The chatter lessens. The odors slither out of my brain, through my nostrils, and back into their dark dens. I'll turn the sensors up again soon, but for now, I need a buffer from the noise. How do humans deal with this every day?

I walk and feel buoyant like I'll fly up into the air, out into orbit, and back toward Anthea. I never realized how reassuring gravity felt until I had less of it.

I find the area labeled "Office," and line up behind a mother and her son. The mother is talking with a woman behind the counter as if the counter woman has done something awful to the son and the mother is here to exact revenge. The son shakes his head and stuffs his hands in his pockets, and fixes his eyes on a point on the ground.

I study the mother as I stand in line. There are nearly a dozen tiny symbols on this woman's clothing: Interlocked and opposing *Cs* on her sunglasses and similar *Bs* on her handbag. Red soles on her high heels, shoes that are impractical for labor or even walking, really. A horse-drawn carriage on the silk scarf tied around her neck. These logos were rarely on advertisements we used as reference points for our human identities, but I saw them occasionally in the thick-paper magazines and on the "Real Housewives" shows, where women adorn themselves with sparkling clothes and dramatic makeup and yell at each other. General Primicerius, usually so impassive, knows a lot about that franchise. We considered styling Mother after these women, but research revealed that such status signifiers are not universally known or respected.

"Gavin was bullied last year, despite everything I did to help him out of his shell." The mother puts a hand on the boy's shoulder, and he seems to shrink. An impressive illusion for a vertebrate. "I realize that it's partially his father's doing," the mother continues, "when a powerful man makes a *mistake*..."

She clears her throat and leans in, her gaze darting around the room. Colonel Muckinzee says humans pride themselves in concealing their emotions, or even in placing a faux emotion over a real emotion. But this chemical stew that runs through them makes everything so obvious. This mission may be easier than I anticipated.

"...people will talk," mutters the boy. He glances at me, and back at his mother, and then to me again. His shoulders slump forward. "Mom, it's not like everything was perfect before...before Dad did whatever. I just need you to sign the thing to let me go to class at the U on Mondays and Wednesdays. And then you can go home, and I can go to homeroom, and things can be normal."

"Oh, is that all?" the mother says. She smiles at everyone in the room. Even I get a glance. Her eyes are wide and suddenly damp. "Isn't that wonderful that all I have to do is sign this paper and everything. Will. Go. Back. To. Normal." The woman signs the paper and lets it drop on the floor. Before the boy can pick it up, she's gone.

Red-faced, he gives the paper to the woman behind the counter.

"Thanks, honey," she says. "Do you want to sit over on that couch and take a few minutes to review it? I can give you a tardy pass if you need it. It would be a shame to start the first day when your paperwork is such a train wreck. I half understand why some people think about going paperless, if you get my drift?"

I don't understand why he laughs at this, but I applaud the counter woman's environmentalism.

It's my turn. As I step forward, the woman behind the counter looks closely at my face—the first real test of my biosuit, my new Earth skin. How is my hairpiece? I know my braid isn't perfect, since Father's abrupt stop made me bump my head against my headrest. Did I choose the wrong style of makeup? Cat eye, contour, nude lip, retro, Golden Goddess, bold brows, smokey eye, Uptown Girl, natural, clubbing...the permutations of product color and application style are very nearly infinite, and the "right" version shifts every month. How does anyone get anything done on this planet?

She smiles and my whole self—body and biosuit—relaxes. "I don't recognize you, honey, which means you're either Deerdra or Emma. Welcome to Danaville."

I extend my hand. "I'm Deerdra. I am new. I am very happy to make your acquaintance."

She places her free hand over our clasped hands and leans in close. Her nails are short but painted a vivid coral to match her lipstick. No neutrals for her. "Deerdra, you're not from here, are you?"

I take a step back. How does this woman know? "Um…" I say.

"That's what I thought," she says. She pauses for a moment. "It's all in your folder. Homeschooled in New Mexico."

I realize that I've been holding my breath. "Ma'am, yes ma'am," I say. I've reverted back to protocol, slipping out of Deerdra and into Agent Grey. I catch myself at the last second and try to morph my near-salute into a more casual hair adjustment. The bangs are good for something, I suppose.

"Well, I am very happy to make your acquaintance, Deerdra. I'm Mrs. Queen. I have to hand it to the homeschoolers—you kids are always so polite. Nobody ever told me the worst part of this job would be the parents." She glances at the couch, but the boy has gotten up. "Gavin!" she shouts. "Come here a second!"

The boy pauses at the doorway and turns. He looks like he's preparing for some kind of cruelty to be enacted on him.

Mrs. Queen hands me a dossier. "I have your folder all set with everything you need. Your locker is #542. It's down the hall on the right, red section. Your schedule is in the folder." She looks at the boy again. "Gavin, sweetie. This new girl has Calc for first period, too. Can you show her around? Deerdra Grey, Gavin Neary; Gavin, Deerdra. There. You're all set, and I made you both a friend. Deerdra, high school is going to seem a little overwhelming for you for a few days, but if you need anything, I'm here. Have a good day, kiddos—now scat."

Gavin and I are in the hall before it even registers that I could have said no, could have insisted that I walk by myself. Mrs. Queen is a force of nature. I wonder if General Primicerius knows any of her techniques.

"So," he says, "Hey. Um. Should we pretend this was our idea and we're not both kind of terrified of Mrs. Queen? Even though we're both kind of terrified of Mrs. Queen?" He extends his hand. "Hey. I'm Gavin."

I stare at the hand. They are such ugly creatures, with their stubby little tentacles, their vestigial claws, all wrinkles and hairs and uselessness. I look at the boy. I mark his longish hair, short, compact nose, the soft hairs on his lip just turning dark. Unlike his mother, he's only wearing one logo—an emblem I recognize from the Marvel universe. One of the extraterrestrial characters, in fact. He notes my hesitancy and drops his hand. He turns away.

"Wait," I say, trying to remember how they introduce themselves. I'm failing my first test. I hold out my hand. "I'm Deerdra," I say. "I am new. I am very happy to make your acquaintance."

The boy's lips and brows crinkle a bit as we shake hands. Can he sense that I'm different? Or am I not accounting for his slower thought processes? Maybe it just takes humans longer to think complete thoughts.

After all, I think, as Gavin and I merge into the flow of bodies headed to classes: they are just cows.

Chapter 4
Slightly Above Average

Gavin is surprisingly helpful. He says he has a cousin who was homeschooled and promises to get me through my first day. He teaches me the seating conventions at Danaville High. Don't sit in the front row (too eager), the back row (too lazy), or the absolute middle of the room. (Which seems like it's the perfect solution. But apparently it's too perfect?) Second or third row in, second or third row back. Two of the Populars from outside are in this class, as well—the Alpha and the dark-haired Popular. They sit in the back of the room and spend the hour alternating between listening to the teacher and picking at their phones.

Gavin's strategy gets me through the rest of the day unnoticed, other than roll call. A few of the more eager teachers made us do something called "icebreakers." Based on the banality of the questions versus the nervous reactions of some of the students answering them, this may be some form of covert psy-op. But I am a trained agent, and I handled them well.

"I am Deerdra. I am new. I like donuts, drawing, and Detroit." "I am Deerdra. My favorite thing I did this summer was travel. From New Mexico, which is where I am from. I am new." "I am Deerdra. A fun fact about me is I am new."

Easy.

I think my biosuit glitched at lunch. My tactical plan suggested I find a table of friendly-seeming girls with an empty seat. When I walked into the lunchroom, my sympathetic nervous system overreacted. Instead of sitting, I kept walking until I found a sunny corner of the atrium. I don't think I could've eaten like a human even if I wanted to. I needed to absorb some sunlight and create my energy in a familiar way. Home cooking, if you will.

So: mostly easy.

Soon it's the last period: Physical Education. Mrs. Queen's dossier includes a bright green sheet of paper with another locker number and combination, and a list of procedures for the class. *No street shoes. No gum or candy. No jewelry. Long hair must be worn up. Adhere to the dress code.*

It's a relief. Nothing about the day has been particularly challenging, but it will be nice to blend in. Eschew individuality and strive toward a common goal. Physical Education seems perfectly structured to avoid politics and pressure. What a wonderful idea.

I walk into the girls' locker room and stop, briefly, as a cloud of shower steam and aerosolized polymers from a dozen hair products rushes past, trying to outpace the voices bouncing against the walls behind it.

But that's impossible. It's just water vapor, probably drawn out by a difference in air pressure or a draft too light to register on my biosuit. Simple physics. So why does this feel so ominous?

The final bell pushes me inside. I have five minutes to change and get into the gymnasium. I make my way to my locker, carefully following Protocol 814.906W for Nudity > Human > Female-Identifying > Adolescent > American > Non-Procreative > Semipublic > Changing Garments.

The protocol for when and how humans reveal their bodies is one of the most complex social standards we have to navigate. Their brains are sophisticated enough to attempt to contain the instinctual drives of their bodies, but not so sophisticated that they can restrict these drives to a designated time. The procedures are endlessly convoluted based on place, partners, and end goal.

Studying their popular culture has been frustrating. A movie opens with a Christmas tree and ends with a woman who owns a small business and a handsome widower kissing chastely under the mistletoe, and another ends with a bloodied lawman kissing his ex-wife as the employees of Nakatomi Plaza look on, while another ends with the local hero kissing his wife as their town conspires to subvert his looming embezzlement charges. I've heard there are other movies, but Mother and Father only watch them after I'm asleep, every other Friday night. They must be classified.

When in doubt, protocol is to stare at the floor and avoid eye contact, while not seeming "weird about it." I want to peek. I want to know if the styling on my biosuit matches their bodies. Did we get it right? Is there anything strange about my biosuit, or is it average? And then there's fashion. There were thousands of choices in underwear alone. Did I pick the right thing for the girl I'm supposed to be? The girl my mission demands? But instead, I keep my eyes down, find my locker, and spin the combination.

There's nothing in there. No regulation uniform. No five-inch shorts and plain T-shirt without logos, as specified in the dossier. I had assumed they would be provided. On my planet, the sarisuits are sourced from a single manufacturer and updated annually. A committee decides on the color and styling, and everyone receives their new garments on the first day of the year. All the cloth comes from one dye lot, so there's no color variation. What's the point of a regulated uniform code if you cannot ensure true uniformity?

The girls leaving the locker room are wearing leggings and Spandex shorts and tank tops and sweatshirts, and nobody seems to care about protocol.

I glance at a tall brunette with a locker near mine, wearing mesh-sided leggings and a sleeveless shirt with the school's volleyball logo on the chest. Her uniform is noncompliant, but at least she is clothed. I can address her with minimal social awkwardness.

"Excuse me? Hello. I am Deerdra. I am new. I am very pleased to make your acquaintance."

She turns toward me, and her face is familiar. The dark-haired Popular. Again. Our Math teacher called her Zoe. AP Calculus and on the volleyball team? Could she be a hybrid of Popular, Brain, and Jock? If she's so talented, why isn't she the Alpha?

"Mmhmm." She doesn't stop adjusting her hair even though the ponytail is nearly perfect. Her hair is so bouncy and shiny, like the ads. I glance in the mirror and see the wisps of hair that have escaped my braid over the course of the day, the little flyaways that pop up when it's humid.

I should file a complaint with the quality assurance division of the biosuit team. I did not, in fact, get slightly above-average hair.

"Yes. Hello. As I said, I am new, and I thought uniforms would be provided. I don't have anything to wear. Do you…do you know what I should do?"

"Be better prepared?" She still doesn't look at me. "Or just grab something out of the loaner bag, I guess." She finally runs her eyes from the top of my head down to my toes as she walks away. I search for a microexpression, a curled lip or a smiling eye or something, anything, to tell me what she's thinking, but her face stays completely neutral.

I can't get a tardy, not on my first day. I scan the locker room and see a bright yellow sign above a bin:

LOANERS
We once were lost, but now we're found,
(Maybe balled up on the ground?)
If you forgot your clothes for track,
Wear us, wash us, and bring us back!

Not the work of a professional poet, but it gets the point across. I riffle through the bin and find a shirt and shorts that are my size. The shorts are, in fact, perfectly regulation: plain black, five inches long, no zippers or adornments. The shirt is a plain heather-grey V-neck, but with a small smiley face embroidered on the pocket. Not code, but it will have to do. Better than being tardy. I pull on the new clothes, lock my locker, and head out into the gymnasium.

Chapter 5
Partners?

The first few minutes of gym class are familiar. The teacher takes attendance and runs through the rules of class. Call him Coach K. *Participate. Be a team player. Hydrate. No street shoes.* Coach K is adamant about the street shoes. He shows us black marks on the floor from previous street shoes. The marks will not come out until the floor is refurbished, and do you know what the state's education budget looks like? Coach K suspects he will be forced to refurbish the floors himself. Maybe Coach K will make us do it and call it a karate unit. *Sand the floor. Sand the floor.* Coach K frowns when nobody responds to this, says our parents would think that was funny.

Coach K watches the same movies as Colonel Muckinzee.

"But this isn't film appreciation," he says. "It's gym. So everyone grab a partner, and let's play some badminton! Two-on-two! Ladder tournament! Serve switches with every point. Volley back and forth until the shuttlecock"—giggles from the class—"very mature, ladies and gentlemen, the *birdie*, then, hits the ground or goes out. After ten minutes, the team with more points goes up a court. Team with fewer points stays put. Whoever's in the top court stays there until they're defeated, then it's back down to the bottom rung and you can work your way back up again. Bootstraps! Character building! All of that fun stuff. Got it? Good. Pair up, head out, and Coach K will get some music going."

How do I find a partner? Nobody has seen me play—how will they know about my skills? As the leader, Coach K should have done a pre-assessment and matched complementary skillsets together. Then the matched pairs would compete, finding the optimal combination for career training.

I was at the top of my class in rote memorization, observation and reporting, linguistics, and the scientific method. It compensated for my weaker skills in problem-solving and improvisation. Ideally, I'd be paired with a counterpart with these strengths for my mission.

Eunice Tiffany's scores in both of these areas were legendary. If things had gone according to plan, she and I would be partners right now. On and off the court.

But she's not here, and I'll have to improvise. Could I pair with someone from one of my earlier classes? There's Zoe, but she's already standing next to the Alpha Popular. They raise their eyebrows at each other and glide off to the field. Who else?

"Hey, Deerdra. You survived your first day as a fightin' Fox?"

"Gavin!" Perfect. "I've made it this far. But this is my first gym class. Organized sports weren't part of homeschooling."

"Consider yourself lucky. Want to be partners?"

"Do you? I wasn't kidding. I've never played badminton in my life."

Gavin smiles at me. "Then maybe for once, I'll be better than one other person. At least for the first few games. Coach K's working on his playbook right now. If we pretend we're trying and let him focus, he'll leave us alone and give us a B-plus."

A B-plus. Slightly above average. "Perfect."

As we walk to the last court, I tip my face up to meet the sun. Our biosuits block the majority of the sunlight from our bodies, so we have to eat food like real humans. But light can still slip through the translucent areas, like eyes and fingernails, and I feel a small surge of energy from this little bit of photosynthesis. I wonder if this is why humans drink coffee.

The first matches start. Badminton is just physics: I know where the birdie will end up as soon as I see the striking angle of our opponent's racquet. After that, all I have to do is put my racquet in the right place and time to return the volley.

I play the game on autopilot and enjoy the sips of energy I'm absorbing. Being outside is such a novelty. I've never known Anthea without the daily air quality scores, and Mother was always cautious. Putting on my air filtration unit was as natural as putting on my shoes.

So being here, on Earth, with its blue skies and green grasses and easy-accessible photosynthesis? When the hardest part of the game isn't hitting the target but avoiding the butterflies that hover overhead? The only true wildlife on Anthea is like Earth's cockroaches—hardened against the elements. Practical, but unattractive. Nothing like these little erratic sky dancers. It's hard to remember to stay slightly above average at badminton. We are ahead 12 to 1 when the whistle blows.

Gavin taps my racquet with his. "You've really never played badminton before?"

"No. Um. I played a lot of tennis in New Mexico, though. It's very similar."

Game two is more of the same. We play against two boys that I recognize from English class. I pull back enough to maintain an easy lead and use my spare energy to watch the other games.

In the court next to us, Zoe and the Alpha Popular are winning, as well. The Alpha is a decent player—nothing showy—but she returns most of the volleys that come her way. Zoe, on the other hand, spikes anything that's shoulder-level and higher. Their opponents, a boy and a girl, are quietly letting the Populars win. A pulled shot here, an underpowered serve there. After Zoe sends one at the other girl's face, the Alpha murmurs a warning "Zo…Derek's not worth it. And **you** broke up with **him.**"

The boy's eyes flick over to the Alpha. "Thanks, Kayla. Zoe, we've talked about this. Leave her alone."

Zoe clenches her jaw and sizzles an overhand across the net.

The whistle blows. The Populars stay in the high court. We start to move up.

Suddenly Gavin says brightly, a little too loud: "I dropped my inhaler. Can you help me find it?" He turns his back to the rest of the group and stares down at the grass. Lowering his voice, he murmurs, "There's not a lot of time to explain, but you don't want to get either of them mad at you. Especially Zoe. Go against one of their group, then they'll all make your life miserable. Kayla used to keep things in check, but she's…she's had a hard year. So this is a really good time to look like we're trying, get that B-plus, and live to fight another day. Cool?"

"Cool. I don't see your inhaler anywhere."

"That's because I don't have one. But apparently, I look like someone who should?" He bends over, calls out, "Found it!" and picks up and pockets a handful of air.

We face off against the Populars. Gavin and I put on a good show, missing shots by inches and just grazing the top of the net on our serves. Zoe's distracted by the boy we just beat—an ex-boyfriend, perhaps?—but Kayla's good at the game and doesn't seem to share Zoe's bad mood.

Coach K's whistle blows. "That's game! Put your equipment away and go change. Grey! Neary! Nice hustle today."

Gavin bobs his head, and a blush works its way up his neck and ears. "Thanks, Coach." He turns to me. "Thanks, Deerdra. See you tomorrow?"

"Yes, you will. We have Calculus together, remember?"

He cocks his head and laughs. "Alright, Homeschool. Later." He jogs off to the boy's locker room. I don't know why he's in such a good mood. According to our research, he'll be facing a gauntlet of towel snapping and pranks. But his microexpressions are the most confident I've seen from him today.

Zoe, however, is in an emotional spiral. Her eyes are pink, and her face is blotchy—physical manifestations of the storm in her brain. Overactive amygdala, weak prefrontal cortex. She needs to find a logical thought pattern and make the prefrontal cortex the primary driver again.

I have the perfect fact for her. Befriending Zoe could help our mission, and even set the standard for Anthean/human interaction in the future.

"Excuse me, Zoe? I couldn't help but overhear what you are going through. May I help?"

Zoe and Kayla turn and look at me. "Okay…"

"In North America, only two percent of high school relationships end in marriage, and half of all marriages end in divorce anyway. Statistically, any relationship you have right now is destined to fail, so it's much more practical to remain single."

Zoe and Kayla both make choking sounds. Zoe spits out a curse word, storms into the locker room, and slams the door. Kayla grabs a hold of my arm and holds me back. The corners of her eyes crinkle. As soon as the door closes, she bursts into laughter.

"Oh my God…oh my God, that was so stupid but so great! She hasn't shut up about Derek all day, and there's literally no reason why she should care. I have no idea why you said that, but that was amazing." She wipes tears out of her eyes and giggles again. "Zoe's going to be pissed, though. You should stay out here for a minute, and I'll go in and handle her. Who are you again?"

"I am Deerdra. I am new. I am very pleased to make your acquaintance."

I extend my arm for a handshake. As Alpha Popular, I'm sure Kayla is accustomed to a more formal greeting than the average student. Kayla's laughter hitches, stops. She turns pale and stares at my chest. This is socially unacceptable, but maybe this is another rite as Alpha Popular, like a threat assessment? Or is something wrong with my torso design?

"Deerdra, where did you get that shirt?"

Ah. It's not my anatomy, just my clothing. "From the loaner bin. I thought uniforms would be provided, but they weren't, so I had to borrow this for the day."

"Oh." The crinkles move from the corners of Kayla's eyes to a furrow in between them. She runs her hand down her hair a few times in rapid succession. "Hey, this is going to sound weird, but can I have that shirt after you change? It belongs to a friend."

The contract above the loaner clothing was quite specific. "I'm sorry, but I need to wash and return it. Rules are rules, and I am trying to stay out of trouble. I am new."

Kayla bites her bottom lip and bounces up and down on her toes. "It's just an ugly shirt from the lost and found. Nobody's going to miss it. Just…just let me have it."

"I can't." I'm losing whatever ground I made with Kayla. I can't tell the Commander that I dismantled a potential friendship with the Alpha Popular over a gym shirt. "You could tell your friend that I found her shirt, and I can clean it tonight and give it to her tomorrow?"

Her nostrils flare, and she looks away, blinking rapidly. "Forget it."

And now Kayla's eyes are pink, Kayla's skin is blotchy, and she pushes past me to get into the locker room.

I don't understand why she's so upset over a shirt. Is it valuable? I check the embroidery on the pocket—maybe it's an up-and-coming brand?—and that's when my fingers notice the texture difference. Below the smiley face, stitched in thread that's the same shade of grey as the shirt, is a name.

EUNICE

Chapter 6
Report

That evening, I compare the replicated version of the Eunice shirt against a scan of the original, which we're keeping to test and log into our system. The initial findings are unremarkable: sebum, loamy clay, some plant matter. In other words, a sweaty, used gym shirt. Mother, ever the scientist, always confident there's more to learn, will run more tests.

For now, she watches her mandated pop culture hour and takes notes. Father sits at the table and reviews my daily briefing. The dueling lizard-claw scuttle of pens is such a small sound compared to how much work is being done.

Father looks up over the rims of his glasses. To keep with his older and slightly-below-average Earth identity, his biosuit worsens vision, and the glasses correct it again. I wonder if he misses his original sight, or if the biosuit vision feels normal now.

"I modified a few things: I know I encouraged you to use colloquialisms, but I'm not sure 'My day was fine' is an acceptable way to address the Colonel. Tomorrow, I would like you to focus more on befriending the Populars and less on this Gavin. I do not see the value in befriending someone with such low social status. But all in all, I am pleased, and I am sure our leadership will be pleased, as well. You followed protocol, remained undetected, and you have reported the facts with care." He glances over at Mother, who has paused her program and is scribbling calculations in the margin of her notes. "You've found something?"

Mother pushes her hair back behind her ears. "This is the third show in a row where the house hunter says they absolutely need an eight-burner stove. The average household size is 2.54 and falling. How much food are they making? Did we miscalculate their daily caloric needs? What are they doing with eight burners at every meal?"

Father looks concerned. "That…that would impact a great many plans. Deerdra, we will verify tomorrow's mission plan against the guidebook and have your orders ready at breakfast. I will send your report to the Colonel myself. Good work today, Agent Grey. Day one is complete."

I'm suddenly so tired that I can barely stand. I wish Mother and Father a good night. Instead of returning my salute, they pull me close and knead my forehead. I am off the clock and am just their daughter once again.

Upstairs, I finally remove my constricting first-day outfit and silently thank whoever decided that pajamas are an acceptable garment for relaxation and rest. At least I'll spend a third of my time on Earth in comfort, even if I'm asleep. I tend to my biosuit and mentally run through my actual day versus the report I handed to Father.

My report is factual, but is it accurate? It's impossible to describe everything about my day. Like Gavin. After watching him and his mother in the office, I assumed he'd be a boring pushover. Gifted enough to take a few college classes, but even a clever cow is still a cow.

But Gavin was...kind. Funny. Perceptive enough to notice that I was a little bit different but empathetic enough to give me a chance. It was nice to begin my day and end my day with him.

I stare at myself in the mirror, finally able to just...be. The clothing and hairstyle and makeup and gestures and body language never end. Be unique but not weird. Unless weird is your thing. Be smart but don't seem too smart. Be fashionable but make it seem effortless. Keep your facial expression neutral-positive. My human classmates will never know what a burden this is—they all breeze about their day knowing exactly who they are, and exactly how to look and act. Knowing their purpose.

I extinguish the light on the bedside lamp and lie down. Sleep, thankfully, is a thing that Antheans and humans have in common.

Chapter 7
Totes McGoats

I wave goodbye to Father and feel a rush of air as a red coupe passes fast and close.

"Hey." Gavin moves from the curb and stands alongside me, watching the car disappear. "Sorry you didn't have a chance to see my mother again, but her social engagements are so pressing. If she doesn't get her space in Aqua Tabata, she's intolerable for the rest of the day."

This is sarcasm. I think. Although based on my first impression, it's hard to believe that Gavin's mother would be tolerable even if she had her preferred space at…Aqua Tabata? I'll research it on my own rather than including it in my report. Colonel Muckinzee is so eager for new cultural data that he will assign new duties without dropping current assignments, and Mother's days are busy enough.

The Unpopular from yesterday is here, chaining her bicycle to a rack. She looks at us and smiles. "Hey, Gav. Where's Heather rushing off to this time? Dermatologist? Psychiatrist? Pedicure? Aura reading? Private eye?"

Her updo is messy, but I can't tell if it's because of the ride or if it's purposely askew. She wears a black shirt with a low back, ripped blue jeans, and a pair of sandals like those worn on *Welcome Back, Kotter*. (One of Colonel Muckinzee's favorite examples of youth culture, the show was removed from our reference library after we realized the actors in that show could now be the grandparents of my peers. Human culture changes quickly even though the colonel claimed the lessons taught on the show were eternal.) Her nails are painted a dark forest green, but almost half of the polish is chipped off. Her makeup is possibly Retro Glam—red lips and black eyeliner. Instead of carrying a backpack, her books are in a reusable shopping bag. It has a drawing of a ruminant carrying a bag over its shoulder, with TOTES MCGOATS written underneath. That goat's bag also has a bag-carrying goat, and a TOTES MCGOATS, and *that* tiny goat also has something on its tiny shoulder.

I will never find this bag, or this girl, in a Sunday advertisement. She is bright and chaotic, and she doesn't match any of my predetermined groups. I think I would like to be her friend. I imagine the Colonel will disapprove.

"Heather's off to the gym to fight the grim specter of death," says Gavin. "I guess if she stays a size four, nobody will blame her for Dad? I don't know. I don't ask. Nice bag. Have you met Deerdra?"

"Hey. You're new, right?" She nods in my direction.

I extend my hand. "I am Deerdra. I am new. I am very…"

"Okay, what is that?" Gavin breaks in. "I know you were homeschooled, but I swear you said the exact same thing to me and Mrs. Queen and a few people in Calc."

"…very cold. Today. It is colder here than it was in New Mexico. Where I am from."

Excellent. The weather is one of the top five emergency conversational topics in our training manual. Weather, the local sporting team that is currently in season, politicians (adults only), things that are directly within line of sight, and future meals.

"Nice," says Barb. "I have an aunt who lives in Santa Fe. She loves it there. We spent spring break with her last year. I ate so many tacos—they're like a totally different food than what you get here. The tacos here are just as bland as everything else. So how did you wind up in Danaville?"

"Father got a promotion and we moved this summer. Mother said she wants us both to make new friends, so I am going to school, and she is exploring her options."

"Gavin's dad explored his options…" Barb waggles an eyebrow and bumps Gavin with her hip.

"Shut up, Barb."

This is playful banter! Each party pretends to feel disdain for the other party, but it's a way to express mutual affection. We had assumed that this was a creation of their fiction writers. There is no benefit to this activity. Clear communication, based on fact and restrained of emotion, is optimal. Fewer mistakes are made, goals and outcomes are expressed clearly, and it's less likely for someone to be at a disadvantage due to differing frames of reference.

But they are both smiling, and their gaits are loose and easy as we walk up the stairs. Barb and Gavin spar and discuss their first day of classes and make half-statements that must be about other students. I drift along beside them, smiling when they smile and making proper affirmative noises at the proper times.

Barb digs through her bag as we walk, removing and returning pens and tampons and receipts and even, I believe, a small yo-yo. Eventually, she finds a lipstick and hands it to me.

"Here. This one worked for me when I was a brunette, but it's terrible now that I'm blonde. Anyway. This will look good on you—your eyes are crazy pretty."

This lipstick contains millions of foreign bacteria and fungi. Enterococcus faecalis, Staphylococcus, Aeromanas. We have engineered my biosuit to withstand any of these, and our scientists don't believe we're susceptible to human diseases, but still. She basically just handed me a petri dish.

But it's a petri dish in an intriguing shade of pink. A little more intense than what the Sunday advertisement girls would wear. There's no way Mother or Father would have let me wear this out of the house—it could attract undue attention. It could make me slightly more memorable. But really, wouldn't refusing a gift from a potential friend cause undue attention? Wouldn't citing a relevant bacteriology study from the *Journal of the American Medical Association* be atypical?

I smear on the lipstick and check my reflection in a window. It's different. The comfortable uniformity of my Anthean sarisuit suddenly feels further away, and I don't know if that's thrilling or terrifying.

"See? Love it. I've never seen anyone with eyes like yours. They're creepy in the best way. *Now* you're ready for Danaville. Keep that, go to class, don't talk to anyone if Gavin doesn't talk to them, too. He and I are the best people in this shithole, so you're lucky that we found you."

She air-kisses at us and breezes away. Gavin smiles. "And that," he says, waving his arm at the empty space in her wake, "was Barb."

Chapter 8
The Home Room

The second day of school is much like the first, and then the third is like the second, and soon the first week of the mission is over. I try to accomplish something mission-oriented every day. I've developed a positive relationship with the regional chain of command. (Mrs. Queen, after all, works in the principal's office and shouts "DEERDRA! COME AND CHAT, HONEY" whenever she sees me.) I'm updating our reconnaissance information to account for modifications to the field terrain. (Sometimes, I use a different bathroom or walk in a new hallway and compare it against the blueprints we have on file. I've added a number of potted plants to the document. They also removed a bench.) Father thinks the Colonel may give me a commendation for my work in enhancing interspecies communications via introduction of advanced technologies. (I lent Kayla a pencil after her lead broke, and then told her to keep it. My pencil was mechanical, and she normally uses a plain yellow number two.)

Every day I look for new evidence of Eunice Tiffany. There's an American chestnut tree dedicated to her in one of the Green Team gardens. "For your work with Danaville's native plants and animals: thank you for protecting those without a voice." I also found her on the drama department's photo wall. Eunice in the school musical, wearing so much stage makeup that she might as well be wearing a biosuit on top of her biosuit. I think she's supposed to be an elderly character—ashy foundation, circles under her eyes—but she looks more like a ghost.

Or maybe I'm projecting. Eunice is my ghost. Our house is the same house. The missing girl lived in my room before she went missing. We still don't know why she went missing.

I try not to think about this, try to focus on the training, the mission, the goal. Our dying planet. But still, when I walk in the door, I can't help thinking that she walked in this door, she dropped her same books by these same stairs. She walked down into the basement to the regeneration room. She needed it like I need it now, like they told us we would even as they were telling us not to use it too much, to keep in mind that we have a mission and it's not comfort, it's not home. Not a spa day, but a dental cleaning.

I try to remind myself of all of this, and then I drop my bag by the stairs and I practically float down, already relaxing. The air gets cooler, closer to the gas mixture on Anthea. The respirators on my biosuit slow, their usual whispering only perceptible now that they're silenced.

The door opens, and a push of cold air comes out. It's dark inside, the corners glowing pink like the sky I'm used to. A hand touches my arm, and I jump. "Mother?" I say. There is an unfamiliar smell, and I make a note that I'll have to find out what it indicates.

"I will leave you," she says and moves past.

I turn and watch her walk up the stairs, expecting her to turn, to come back, to ask me about my day and why I need the room so early in our mission, but she does none of these things, just continues slowly up the stairs. Once again, I feel the gravity in every footstep, and then I feel the cold air pulling me in, and I move into the room.

I shut the door behind me and twist the lock. I take off the shoes that have been holding me down, take off the dress and the undergarments and the socks. I turn the knob.

It is just like they have told us it would be. It's like home. I rise slowly, feeling the gravity leave me, my bones, the shell I have to wear here, feel it all slipping away like mist.

Under my biosuit, my skin swells as the cells devour the micronutrients missing in the Earth atmosphere. If there were cosmetics ads on Anthea, I would be moving from "before" to "after." I would be the girl with the knowing smile and the flawless skin. Easy and breezy. I lie back and let the room take me away.

Home. Our dying planet. Eunice Tiffany, the missing girl who has taken up so much of my energy here, would have floated in this same room. I wonder what her first days of school were like—was she sad or happy—did she fit in? How was she friends with Kayla, the Alpha Popular, when I've only befriended Barb and Gavin? While I know they're above average, I also know that's not how they appear in the hierarchy. The Colonel wouldn't be impressed.

I try to put it all out of my mind and just float, just feel home. The clock ticks down. We have been told we cannot use this room for more than a half-hour every week.

We have all learned the story of Family 9, who became addicted. Their reports slowed, contact became intermittent, and then finally stopped. By the time a rescue crew could be sent, it was too late: they were found here in this room, after their biosuits were welded to their actual bodies as their skin cells tried to slake their thirst for nutrients. We have seen the images of them in this room, all of them bunched together and floating, smiles on their dead faces.

"It is important that you use this room and important that you do not use it too much," Colonel Muckinzee said. "Take advantage of your time here. Relax. Remember your mission. Remember your home."

Again, I try to make my mind go blank, to focus on the grey-pink glow, identical to our sky. The sky on Earth is obscene, bright, and blue, like everything too much and too little at the same time. I can't believe I ever thought it was pretty. I whisper the word. "Home…home…home." I allow myself to float upward, imagine that I'm blending into that pink horizon, that my Earth skin is misting into nothing as I float. And then I see them. At first, I think they are stars, but we haven't seen stars in the Anthean sky for decades. I've only heard about them in school, seen the images in textbooks. I float closer and put my hand on the wall. They are written in pencil, a series of circles, like balloons, like a constellation. One word is written underneath in handwriting I recognize from the missing girl's things: "Jerkhin."

Chapter 9
What is it About This Janitor?

"Deerdra!"

It sounds like Barb. I think? But I can't see her anywhere.

"Deerdra!"

I nearly lose the apple off of my lunch tray when I finally see her. Barb is sitting at the end of the cheerleader's table. Her messy updo has been transformed into a sleek ponytail. Her lips are sticky and pink. She's wearing a men's jacket with a large "J" embroidered on the front breast pocket.

She looks like a prototype of a wholesome, preppy teenager. She radiates invisible pleated skirts and megaphones and spirit fingers.

"Barb? You're a cheerleader?"

"Ha. Hell, no. But it's easy to fake the look. Listen, can you help me?"

"Of course. How may I assist?"

"Jerkoff's after me."

I thought I knew this euphemism, but there is no evidence of that activity happening here. That activity would stand out.

"What? Who is…Jerkoff?"

"Jerkoff. Mr. Jerkhin, the janitor. I borrowed some paper from the vice principal's office, and he freaked out."

Jerkhin. The same name that was written on the ceiling.

"If he catches me, I'm getting detention," Barb continues. "It's just paper! Can you take my bag over to the commons, and I'll meet you there in like five minutes? I need to perform some evasive maneuvers. I swear he can track like a basset hound."

"No. That's a bad idea."

"Come on, Deerdra, I thought you had a little maverick in you…"

"No. I'll help. But the commons is a bad idea. It's public, centrally located, and can be accessed by six different hallways. There's a high probability Mr. Jerkhin will go there multiple times if he's canvassing this area."

Barb grins, exposing front teeth stained faintly with this morning's red lipstick. "You're amazing, D. Here—my bag's under this coat."

I take the bag, and we start walking toward a row of doors, but she grabs me and pulls me down. "Hit the brakes!" Through the glass, we see the janitor walking down the adjacent hall. She giggles and cuts her eyes back and forth. "He flew on by. Good. I feel like I'm in a spy movie."

"Over here," I say, pointing toward a little alcove on one end of the cafeteria. "Every blueprint I've seen has a door right…" There are some leftover theater sets and paint cans. But no door.

"Well, it's not. But"—Barb perks up and glances at me with a curious smile—"when we get out of this, you're telling me about these blueprints."

"The door should connect to the backstage area of the small auditorium. That should be how they move the sets on and offstage."

"They got rid of the little theater like ten years ago and turned the space into overflow storage for sports equipment. It's all football pads and jock straps in there."

Barb grabs my hand and hauls me down next to her behind a large canvas flat painted with a cityscape. Mr. Jerkhin walks past the alcove. His eyes scan the cafeteria, and Barb is right—he really does seem to smell the air. But that's impossible—he's a human, not an animal. I've watched too many nature documentaries. Mr. Jerkhin probably has a cold or is allergic to the dust that he disturbs as he cleans the school.

He moves with a shambling lurch that seems like he's a half-second from falling over, like his top half weighs more than it should and it's pulling him down. His head waves back and forth as his black eyes suck an enormous amount of data out of the room. His body is lumpy, but he doesn't seem dense or fat—he's strangely fluffy, like his coveralls are stuffed full of marshmallows. I want to poke his belly to see if he giggles like that sentient biscuit dough.

I snicker at the thought, drawing a glare from Barb. But really, it's all so silly—I'm light-years away from my home. I survived interstellar travel. I'm trying to find out what happened to my predecessor, who used to live in my very bedroom, but I have no idea why this one terranaut matters so much to the General and the Colonel and even the Council. My planet is dying. And now I'm trying to avoid engagement with a custodian, crouching in the dark in this dirty, neglected space, inhaling paint fumes and aerosolized chicken sandwich oil and some old, sour, organic smell.

That last smell. Sweat. I'm smelling sweat. Layers of it. Whole generations of it. Which means the wall between us and the equipment storage locker isn't as solid as it seems. I turn around slowly, so as not to draw Mr. Jerkhin's attention, and examine the wall. What I thought were drywall seams have small hinges. This wall is a partition—the individual panels can accordion together and push to one side to create one large space. And there, on the innermost panel, is a small, recessed handle. Easy to miss when you're looking for a standard door.

Mr. Jerkhin lurches methodically around the lunchroom, like an old shark moving through a beachhead, looking for just the right morsel.

"Seriously?" Barb whispers. There's a fear in her voice that I haven't heard before. What is it about this janitor that has both of us spooked?

I use two fingers to point toward my eyes, then out toward the cafeteria. I've seen the gesture in so many movies, and I've been dying to use it. It draws a smirk, but Barb scans the cafeteria as I reach up, find the catch, and open the door a crack. We slither through the opening and ease the door closed again.

Chapter 10
X-Files Stuff

My first thought is: we made it!

My second: it smells even worse in here.

Looking around the equipment room, I'm reminded of how fragile humans are. Most of the other life on this planet has physically adapted to their environments, growing shiny carapaces or sharp talons, or at least some passive camouflage. Here, rows of hockey pads and helmets wait at attention, ready to defend soft, pink bellies and delicate brain tissue. You could cobble together an army of humanoid exoskeletons with all of this equipment.

Barb freezes and stares forward. Then she bounces on her toes, her arms stretch out, then up, and she dives onto a large, cushy mat lying in a corner. A cloud of dust puffs up into the air. This room hasn't been disturbed in a while. We're safe. In that case, blend in. Follow suit. Build trust.

I splay out like a starfish and flop back on the mat. It's nearly a meter thick, and the spongy foam wraps around me before popping me back up to the surface. Barb laughs and then claps her hand over her mouth. We don't want to attract Jerkhin. This is still a covert operation.

For a while, the two of us bounce around, enjoying the freedom from gravity and the illicit silence that we have to preserve. Barb's eyes glow with delight. Eventually, we settle in. Sunbeams stream through a high window, highlighting motes of dust that we've disturbed. We lie quietly for a moment, watching the tiny specks glimmer in the light and disappear again. Over sixty tons of cosmic particles fall to Earth every day, cast off from comets and meteorites and other bits from other planets. Even other galaxies. They blend with pollen and dander and Earth soil, drifting about and eventually settling on flat surfaces as everyday Earth dust. I'm not the only alien thing in this room.

If it weren't for the smell, this would be a comfortable place. It's warm and quiet, and the mats hug us close.

"Barb?"

"Yeah?"

"What just happened? With you and the janitor?"

Barb's nose wrinkles, and her eyes roll slightly. Classic microexpressions for disgust. "I hate that guy. He's so creepy. Well, not creepy, exactly, just…blank. Most of the staff and the teachers here have at least some personality. You can joke with them or talk about the weather or something."

The weather! One of our top five emergency conversational topics. How many hours of human-terranaut interaction went into that one line in our manual? The researcher who uncovered that detail should be proud—decades later, a member of a constantly changing demographic still uses it as an emergency communication strategy.

"But it's like Jerkhin has this sense for whenever anyone wants to have any fun, and he's there. Just…staring. If you break a rule, he'll rattle off the exact bylaw that you broke. It's just creepy."

"There's a bylaw against using school supplies? You borrowed some paper."

"Welllll…the paper had already been used."

"Then there's a bylaw against reusing paper? That seems wasteful."

"Still being used, then."

Barb reaches into the TOTES MCGOATS bag and removes an accordion folder stuffed with paper. It's labeled EUNICE TIFFANY.

I've stared at this name on our own dossiers. I have read her Council file, her training materials, the reports she dutifully sent back on high school social norms, soil samples, crop rings, the contaminants in the air and water. But I've never seen this particular dossier, and the fact that it exists means something, something big, but I'm not quite sure what it is yet. "The missing girl," I say. "But what is…"

"Okay here's the weird part," Barb says. "There are two of these in the building. One was in the vice principal's office. Was." She points to the folder. "It was in Mrs. Queen's drawer, which is weird, but whatever, vice principal's office. Hence the cloak and dagger operation," she says, as if this was enough of an explanation, as if it explained anything at all.

"And the other?"

"This is the super weird thing," she says. "The other is in the janitor's office."

"How do you know that?" I say.

She gets serious, lowers her voice. "I think he had…I don't know…something to do with it. Something. They were, like, friends? Which doesn't make any sense even if he didn't look like himself and Eunice didn't look like Eunice, you know what I mean?" She doesn't wait for a confirmation. "So even though nobody else seems to think he's a suspect, he's a suspect to me. I've watched enough TV to know that when a guy who looks like that takes an interest in a girl who looks like Eunice, and then that girl goes missing? Come on."

"Interesting," I say. This explains his name written on the ceiling.

"So you've heard about it?" Barb says.

I need to be careful here. Our social scientists still haven't been able to document how humans respond to controversial topics when dealing with their superiors. Their concept of friendship reduces even the most-researched theories to mere guesswork. There are unique responses for an infinite number of variables.

"A little? I just know the name and that she went missing. Or died. And it was…"

"Weird. Crazy. X-Files stuff."

"X-Files stuff," I say, and I cannot hide the disgust in my voice. We have watched this show, of course. It was Colonel Muckinzee's favorite to, as he said, "hate watch." A tub of zoogli and the X-Files was an excellent evening for the Colonel.

"An explosion at the dairy? Really?" Barb says. "An explosion large enough to wipe out twenty acres? The FBI called in because of a new strain of dairy cultures? Dairy cultures! Come on, dude. No way."

"I don't know much about dairies. They didn't have them in New Mexico, of course. My family…"

"That's another thing," Barb says. "Eunice's family? They just up and move? With Eunice still technically missing? I mean, the FBI said they found a molar. A molar?"

I have held this molar, and I can confirm that it was created as part of Eunice Tiffany's biosuit. I have similar "dental evidence" to be left at the scene of an emergency retrieval. So why wasn't Eunice retrieved?

"We have been told not to worry, that these kinds of things never happen in Danaville. Father's employer was very adamant.

"But here's the thing. Strange things happen here all the time. Stranger than strange. Weird lights. Explosions." She spreads her fingers, and her eyes widen like she's telling a campfire story. She's enjoying this, but she's serious underneath the showmanship. "The freakin' FBI sent to investigate a dairy? People just don't want to think about it."

I look around at the sunlight coming in through the high windows, the only semi-ruined blue sky. I am getting used to seeing clouds, stars, their moon. At home, it is all a grey smear, dark and polluted. Pink around the edges for a few brief minutes at sunrise and sunset, but overall: ruined. Dying. "But it's nice here," I say. "It is really very nice. Maybe even nicer than…New Mexico."

Barb thinks for a moment, her eyes absently scanning the shelves of equipment.

"It's…it's fine here, I guess. If you like picket fences, and people who talk your ear off in the line at the grocery store, and you fit in with what's normal, I'm sure it's great. But when something like Eunice happens, you wonder what's behind all the shiny smiles. When the FBI shows up and everybody is all like, 'oh okay, those dairy cultures sure sound dangerous; let's go to the game and forget about everything for a while.'"

"Does the game matter?"

"Right?" Barb says as if I have made a salient point. I'm hoping for a context clue because I have no idea which of their infinite games she's referring to. It's not The Big Game—that's in the first few months of the year. Not the rapper. Could I have just lost The Game by thinking about the game? That was popular for a while. Board games, ball games, Game of Thrones, game of love, mind games… It must not matter since she's still going.

"…say they're on the case, but they've never talked about who did it or why. Not that the Danaville police crack many cases that involve more than speeding or drunk and disorderly. But still."

I just nod. She's on a roll.

"After the candlelight vigil and the thoughts and prayers, everything pretty much went back to normal. And that's the thing!" She leans forward, body tensed and face flushed. She hauls the dossier out of the shopping bag, and it thuds on the mat between us. She cares about this, maybe more than even she knows.

"Eunice. Wasn't. Normal. She was beautiful, of course, anyone could see that. And brilliant. And her family was rich."

What? I'd always assumed she had the same slightly-above-average directive as I did. But Barb continues before I can formulate a question.

"I was all set to hate her, but she was just so nice! She was genuinely interested in people. She joined the drama club, but she didn't audition for the first term—Ms. Moore would have made her the lead in a second. But Eunice joined the crew and did sets and talked to whoever wasn't on stage. You always could tell that she was listening to what you were saying, even if it was just a dumb story about how you hate chicken patties. God, everything in this room smells like sweat and chicken patties. Anyway, you'd think that someone that kind and that smart and that pretty would have a thousand friends, but nobody really…stuck for her. Nobody but Kayla."

"Eunice was supposed to be Popular," I say. I mean it as a question, but it comes out as a statement. The General gave her a better biosuit than me and a better backstory and apparently better interpersonal training. Eunice was designed to be an Alpha.

"Right?" she says again as if I've made some kind of important point. "I never saw Eunice outside of school. Someone like that should be at every birthday party and football game and whatever else people do around here. But after school, she'd just go away. Although, that may have been her family. I've never seen her parents, not even before she was…before all of this. They released a statement after she disappeared, but that's it."

I have read that statement, authored by the Council's crisis communications office.

"After she was…after everything, everyone moved along like nothing happened. Like finding a molar was enough." Barb's voice goes tight. "She was a good person. Someone should care about her, and since her family can't be bothered, I guess it's up to me." She dramatically flops back onto the mat and looks at me, blowing a few stray hairs out of her eyes. "Wow, that was a whole thing, wasn't it?" she says.

I haven't followed protocol for any of this. I should have thought of follow-up questions while Barb talked, to immediately engage her and encourage further detail in the conversation.

"That was kind of a whole thing," I say. Barb laughs and I do, too. I lie back down on the mat next to her. For a moment, I forget that I am a terranaut on a mission, a spy in this high school. I think what I'm feeling is empathy? Whoever designed this updated sympathetic nervous system really did a stellar job. I will note this in my report. "I am sorry, Barb. About everything. I think it's good that you're doing this."

Barb shrugs. Her eyes are damp, but she smiles. The sincerity is retreating, and her shields are going back up. "I mean, what else am I going to do? I don't graduate for twenty-two months and fourteen days, and I feel like 'How I Solved The Disappearance of Eunice Tiffany' would make a pretty strong admissions essay for college. Hopefully qualify for in-state tuition at a school that's far away from here. Hey, what did you think of New Mexico? Do you miss home?"

It takes me a second to parse these two very different locations before I remember that, to Deerdra Grey, New Mexico and home should be one and the same. New Mexico was light years away from home, a brief stop for pre-mission fact-finding. Home is home. "New Mexico was fine. Our town was small, and we only lived there for a few years since we have to move so much for Father's job." Images of Anthea flash through my mind. Sarisuits. Our orderly residential unit.

Pink skies. Respirators. *Time to focus. You must save them.* "Would you really want to move all the way out to New Mexico? Wouldn't you miss it here?"

"I've lived here my whole life, and it's never felt like home. I mean, it's fine. What are the odds that, with billions of people on this planet, everyone is put exactly where they should be when they're born? My family's good, I've got Gavin, and I'll get out of here eventually. This is home for now, but it won't be home forever."

A bell rings and pulls us out of our cozy space. We have ten minutes until the next class period. We tuck the dossier inside a binder labeled "DEFENSIVE PLAYBOOK '98—FIGHT, FOXES, FIGHT."

We walk out of the equipment room and back into the flow of students exiting the cafeteria. I don't see Jerkhin anywhere. We walk in silence. I wish I had something to say. Eunice, apparently, would know exactly what to say. But for now, we let the rest of the herd move us along until Barb stops near the administrative offices.

"I've gotta head down to the art wing. Um—thanks. For keeping me out of trouble. For the talk. Just…for everything. Thanks. If you're early tomorrow, come hang with me and Gav before school starts? We're going to figure out how to tackle that file."

She wraps an arm around my waist and squeezes—my first hug from a human—and walks away.

I believe I have made another friend. Two friends. That's more than Eunice. Maybe I am a better agent. Maybe I'm assimilating better than she did. Maybe I'm more skilled at blending in. Maybe it's time for me to stop reading reports about the local culture and start taking charge. Not usurping my Mission Leader, of course, but at least dropping my trainee status and going to full agent.

Mrs. Queen spots me from her office, gives me a thumbs-up, and grins, showing teeth stained with today's lipstick and a lifetime of coffee. Then she points at her feet, then my feet, back and forth, and gives me another, even more enthusiastic thumbs-up.

I've selected the same practical, sensible shoes as our sixty-year-old secretary.

Back to the reports tonight.

THE FRIENDSHIP PROTOCOL

PROTOCOL 5.1.2J: ESTABLISHING RELATIONSHIPS (SECONDARY) (JUVENILE)

As discussed in Protocol 5.1, humans sort their social classifications using three roughly concentric circles: tertiary (see 5.1.1J/A), secondary (this section) and primary (see 5.1.3J/A).

To move a relationship from the tertiary ring ("acquaintance") to the secondary ("friend"), one should approach existing acquaintances. While some humans have the ability to jump from stranger to friend with near immediacy, it seems to be an extremely recessive trait.

- Shared activities and experiences are a strong bonding agent.
- Small groups in a semi-private location are often a favorable combination.
    - Humans share a hive mind on the proper level of intimacy for friendships.
    - Too public and their neurons become overwhelmed by the potential connections; too private and they may focus on threat assessments.
        - (Statistically, we know that this is illogical as known entities tend to harm each other more than strangers. The prehistoric tendency to mistrust those "not like us" is buried deep in the human brain despite its obvious detriment to society.)
        - Private gatherings may skip from a friendship classification to something more intimate. See 6.1.1J/A. Clearance level Foxtrot required for this section.
- Suggested conversational topics:
    - Current common experiences.
    - Questions about local people, relationships, or locations that would fall between completely unclassified and need-to-know.
    - Keep the conversational focus to roughly equal proportions of you, the subject(s) in the discussion, and other/outer foci. (See your mission details for declassified backstory information.)

WHEN INVESTIGATING INFORMATION PERTINENT TO YOUR MISSION:

- Press the subject as much as seems allowable without seeming suspicious.

- Keep questions defined by a tone of mild curiosity, microexpressions casually interested.
    - Humans will deflect or even close off communications on this subject matter if pressed too firmly but will disclose more as the relationship moves from tertiary toward primary. Learn what you can, but don't burn a potentially level-1 source for level-4 information.

Chapter 11
Do I Miss Home?

After dinner and homework and a few episodes of the Real Housewives with Mother, I can't get to sleep. I keep thinking back to Barb's question: do I miss home?

Of course, I do. Anthea was predictable and familiar. And beautiful, even as the sky grew more ominous. Most Anthean plants use green, red, and blue light evenly, so our forests are shades of grey and brown instead of green. The metallic leaves glitter in the slightest breeze.

Our region is like Earth's deserts, with plant life that matches our more rugged surroundings and, more recently, the state of our sky. The darkening sky has reduced the amount of green light that makes it to the surface. Our plants adapted, only using red and blue wavelengths for photosynthesis. The few plants we have are almost as green as those on Earth.

It's one of the reasons why so many interstellar travelers are from my region. Earlier terranauts from other parts of Anthea had difficulties on Earth, surrounded by seas of green and no familiar metallic sparkle. My family is accustomed to green trees and grasses.

I don't know if I'll ever feel at home under Earth's constantly changing sky. Blue and white, grey and stormy, fire colors at sunrise and sunset, even green on one memorable occasion when the tornado sirens wailed. Stars and planets shining at night. The sky should be nearly unchanging, like the ocean. A hint of pink at the edges at morning and night. That's it. That's home.

At least, I think that's how the skies looked. I spent nearly two Earth years on the ship, staring at research papers and source videos, our small windows looking out into inky-black space. I've forgotten a lot of the small details about Anthea. If we went back today, I don't know where we would live. Our residential unit would have been thoroughly cleaned and then given to the next highest-ranking officer. Someone else has been sleeping in my regeneration pod for nearly two years, while I slept on the ship.

I enjoyed parts of living on ship. It was my first taste of privacy. Instead of using the crew quarters that ringed the vessel, I slept in a converted storage room in the center. Mother insisted. Her father died of a cell mutation—too many trips between Earth and Anthea, brokering peace treaties in the first few years after the Roswell crash, cosmic rays bombarding his DNA with every crossing. Mother is proud that my grandfather was a founding member of the alliances between so many governments. But she wishes she could tell him that, instead of telling me stories about the man in the photos who aged too fast, his skin fading from a lustrous lead grey to powdery pale ecru.

I made that room my own, filling the wall displays with images from my old life and the things from my Earth lessons that piqued my curiosity. At first, it was animals from my nature shows. Would I see an elephant when I was on Earth? Could Mother and Father get me a pet? Investing so much time and money into a creature that has no tangible rewards seemed like such a uniquely human activity. Then the animals gave way to artists. Painters, musicians, actors. These always perplexed Mother and Father because I couldn't explain why I liked the artists I liked. I just…liked them. Van Gogh's wide brushstrokes and heavy paints weren't realistic, but they made me more excited to see Earth's fields and flowers and nights more than any photos did. The same with Hendrix and his guitar. He didn't have the technical precision of other guitarists, and he didn't always follow the other musicians in his band. But when he played, I didn't hear the guitar. I felt calm, cool breezes and warm summer suns and forgot where I was entirely.

Sometimes when I can't sleep here on Earth, I close my eyes and recall the low hum of the engine room, try to see my perfectly curated walls.

And now, Earth. The town of Danaville still feels totally alien to me, but Danaville High is starting to make sense. I was a child when I left Anthea, and now I'm old enough to helm my section of the mission. I'm making an impact. I may be helping my people.

The ship was comforting but temporary. My memories of Anthea are fading.

So do I miss home? Where is my home?

Chapter 12
Mission Leader

I am slow to wake up the next morning. I linger in the shower. Showering is a new experience for me. I'd occasionally use a sonic scrubber to knock the dust off my skin, but our bodies are naturally just cleaner. No hair, no sebum, none of the goo that seeps out of human's pores and ears and eyes and noses without them even noticing. I once saw a man blow his nose into a piece of cloth and then put the cloth back into his pocket. A businessman with a desk job and a pocket full of mucus in a blue bandana. They really are disgusting if you think about it. I am trying not to think about it.

Earth showers are impractical and wasteful, but there's something wonderful about standing in the warm spray surrounded by the bright colors and smells of a flower garden or a bakery. Today, I opt for rose-scented products. According to one of my magazines, the scent encourages friendly emotions in humans. I want to enhance my relationship with Barb and Gavin today. I feel better, more alert, as I head down to breakfast.

"Good morning, Deerdra; goodbye, Deerdra! I'm late for class!" Mother's lips brush the top of my head as she rushes out of her bedroom, nearly knocking me over with her gym bag. She bounds down the stairs, calling in Father's general direction. "Goodbye, my dear. I will send you today's coordinates as soon as I receive them!" The door slams, and her car engine starts.

Father is at the kitchen table, struggling through his breakfast. We don't need to eat—our vitamin regimens and a little sunlight will sustain us—but eating meals helps support our cover identities. If someone glanced in our window on their morning walk, they'd see Father, who is About That Age Where He Should Be Thinking About Those Things, starting the day with oatmeal.

Mother's latest role is Trying To Live Her Best Life. She's off to yoga or spin class almost every morning. At least 70% of her meals have to include something labeled "detox" or "superfood." We think there's a hiccup in the Best

Life scheduling algorithm—between fitness, work, volunteering at my school, meditative self-care, bettering herself, and keeping up on social trends, her daily schedule often lists thirty hours of activity. Her Best Life doesn't seem as fun as it was before. It's hard. I know she enjoys the challenge, and as an agent, she's an excellent role model, but I miss her.

I feel…off today. I can feel Mother's kiss radiating through my entire brain. I can hear Father chewing his oatmeal from across the room. *Slurrrp smack smack smack* and *gchk!* as he swallows. The kitchen's buzzy fluorescent lights accentuate the lines around his eyes and the paunch around his middle. It's a smart part of his disguise—Father's actual body is trim and muscular, but the extra room in his human abdomen gives him an inconspicuous place to hide sensors and equipment. It also helps him with his slightly-below-average persona, helping avert suspicion and making him forgettable as he goes about his covert missions. But this morning, he just looks…sloppy. How can he be the husband of a woman living her best life and the father of an above-average daughter? I wonder if he realizes how much of my work to look like the advertisements is negated by his ill-fitting clothing and dated hairstyle. Then he looks up, sees me, and the tired lines fall away from his face.

"Good a.m., Deirdre! May I serve you a breakfast?" Father rises, pulls a chair out from the table, and grabs an extra bowl from the cupboard.

"Good morning, Father. The term a.m. isn't an acceptable synonym in this instance."

"My studies run counter to that, sweetheart. Tim from Work with Glasses uses them interchangeably. We have a meeting at nine o'clock in the morning, which is nine a.m., and he stated he would see me in the a.m., which is also in the morning. Algebraic property of equality applies. You should add it to your lexicon."

Father's malapropisms usually don't bother me. I don't know why they do today, but they do. Maybe I didn't spend enough time in the regeneration chamber last night.

Or maybe my mission commander should know basic language skills.

"Only my vice principal and Mrs. Queen speak like that, Father."

"Then your vice principal and Mrs. Queen must be keeping it right along on the tightness, Deerdra. I have studied this for longer than you have."

"I'm at school every day! I am immersed in the most cutting-edge popular culture. Please, don't try to be what you're not."

Father half smiles, but a furrow sweeps in between his eyebrows. "I realize I'm not cool, or happening, or whatever the lingo is, Deerdra. That's not my mission. I know enough about human culture to avoid day-to-day suspicion and to successfully interface with my professional contacts. Maybe that's enough."

I almost say nobody even says "lingo" anymore, but he nods his head as if the conversation is over. He sets his spoon on top of the oatmeal, and we watch its slow descent into the sludge. The itch still pulses in my brain, and the last thing I want is for Father to drive me to school. We traveled light years on the ship with no conflict, but I can't fathom the idea of two miles in the car with him right now.

"Maybe. Whatever. I'm walking to school. I need to move Barb and Gavin from tertiary to secondary today, so I should plan. And I haven't filed a supplemental biological report in quite a while."

"Very well, Deerdra. I could also use some additional time this morning." He's all Mission Leader in his delivery. "The General says there's a report of an advance team from the planet Makkel. The Council never approved such a mission. I'm sure it's a simple matter of late paperwork, but still: you will be careful, of course." He shudders. "A lower species, I'm afraid."

"Of course."

"Then I hope your mission goes well. You have always surpassed our expectations as a daughter. Colonel Muckinzee is lucky to have you, and our people are, as well." The Mission Leader softens, and Father takes over. He reaches out to knead my forehead, but I dodge his hand and scoop up my backpack.

"I should go." I want to tell him I'm sorry, that I don't know why I'm so snappish today. But I look at him and the itch throbs through my brain and down my spine. I settle the pack on my shoulders and walk out the door.

Chapter 13
I. See. You.

The walk is quite pleasant. It's slightly cooler than the first week of school, and my biosuit compensates. An ultrasonic frequency excites the carbon nanotubes in my synthetic skin, and soon, I'm warm and toasty again. Still, I make a mental note to bring a sweater tomorrow. Science is efficient, but some of my new sweaters are both practical and aesthetically pleasing. I'd even say cute.

I think about Father's final words. A Makkel in the region. Unbelievable. Makkel is one of Anthea's closest neighboring planets harboring intelligent life capable of space travel. Why would they be on Earth? Do they have similar plans? Or are they watching us, keeping a friendly eye on their neighboring planet?

If there's a Makkel agent assigned to me, they're sure to be bored. I feel like I haven't done much here on Earth. My mission is to find out what happened to Eunice Tiffany, and I'm not sure if I'm closer today than when we arrived.

I put in earbuds and cue up one of my favorite playlists from the ship—my Top 100 list. Early on in our journey, Mother wrote an algorithm to find the best 100 Earth songs written in the last 100 years. It pulled every hit list ever distributed. It searched for magazine articles that ranked songs. It parsed the foundations of the music—how did the key and the time signature and the chord structures interact? In less than a minute, the algorithm gave us a preliminary list of 500 titles. And then the best part—we spent hours in my room, listening to music and just…talking. Beatles or Stones? Britney or Christina? Demi or Selena? What did I like about the songs I liked? Did I like synthesizers or acoustics? Drums? Swing or square tempo?

After every conversation, she'd update the algorithm. She never felt the music as deeply as I did and got a little impatient when I just knew I liked a song for no quantifiable reason. But we kept listening, and she kept updating until it was perfect. My mother is a scientist, and I have always been her favorite experiment.

I enjoy the walk and the music and the air while my biosuit runs a diagnostic. After a few minutes, a report pops up on my phone: all systems operating within normal parameters. Some slight deformation on the skin near my jawline, but a topical cream should repair the damage. It's a reminder to spend the full time allotted in the regeneration chamber instead of leaving early. The damage may be small, but previous missions have found that once one system starts to go, the rest can rapidly devolve. I punch OKAY on the screen. It asks me to take a selfie, which I do. The report and the photo auto-send. Our scientists will use the data for the next generation of biosuits. Colonel Muckinzee will probably have a comment about ways I could improve my hair. He is sure that big, 1980s-style bangs will make a comeback soon. He thinks it's a way for women to nonverbally assert their dominance.

The crisp fall air is shoved aside by an acrid petroleum smell. A rusty pickup truck thunders down the street, belching black smoke and engine noise. Instead of passing me, however, the driver pulls over and sticks his head out of the open window.

It's Mr. Jerkhin, the janitor.

The janitor shouts something that I can't hear over his radio or his inefficient engine and my playlist. I pull out an earbud, and the first thing I realize is that he's also a Johnny Cash fan. The early stuff.

I'm not worried about my safety, since I'm stronger than humans. But this is atypical behavior for an adult. Extremely atypical. This would scare the average high school girl.

"You." Mr. Jerkhin leans haphazardly through the open window, trying to stare me down. He wavers a little and looks down the road at the school, up to the top of an elm tree, at a ladybug crawling on his window.

The street is still. Nobody is coming to save me.

"I see. You," Jerkhin says, stifling a belch. "You think you're. Getting away. With it. But I know. I know what you and the others are up to."

He can't focus on anything, and he can't string a sentence together. His mouth opens and closes like a fish. He's holding his left shoulder, and the arm just falls flat against the truck, bounces as he shouts, more like a pointer than an actual hand. I wonder if he's been drinking. Sometimes the Real Housewives documents similar behavior results from excessive wine drinking. He wasn't acting like this yesterday. He's falling apart at 7:30 in the morning. He must be drunk. I should be able to talk my way through this.

"I don't know what you're talking about, sir. Have we met?"

"Not officially, your majesty." He loops his hand with a flourish. "But I've seen. You. Not YOU, you. You before you. You. Think you're so smart. Smarter than me? You know EVERYTHING, don't you? But you don't know. I know. I KNOW. So when you don't know, you know I know. Just remember that. Be a shame if you got caught."

He smiles ghoulishly, flops his head forward, throws both hands over the wheel, and the truck lurches down the road toward the school.

He knows! I don't know how he found out that I helped Barb steal the file, but I can't let her get caught with it. I grab my phone.

BARB

Hey—wait for me outside. I don't think we should go over those notes this morning.

COME ON. G and I r ready to read!

I know. Just wait.

K. Sup?

B there soon. Will explain

Chapter 14
William and Stefanie Get the Call

Even though they are employed by the same organization, in similar fields, William and Stefanie rarely see each other at work. They like it that way—it's important for them to each have their own identity, and to keep their work-life at work and their private life private. Their current setup is close to perfect: carpool occasionally, a lunch date every other week, and a quick smile when one sees the other's signature at the bottom of a report. They chitchat about their days while making dinner, share the latest office gossip, and then try to forget about the daily grind as they hurry through chores and the last few hours between food and sleep.

This morning is different. Stefanie is at her favorite coffee shop, actually enjoying the way the biosuit feels this morning in her post-yoga glow. She is finishing her usual BLT breakfast sandwich and waiting for her coffee to cool when William calls.

"We're going to need you on this one. Things…may have changed. Dramatically."

She sweeps up the leftover breakfast debris and tosses it into the trash, and grabs her coat and purse just as William's black sedan pulls in front of the shop.

"How bad?" She blinks at the sun that the sedan reflects into her eyes—a little painful, but good pain. She's been inside for far too long.

"Pretty bad."

"Pop the trunk?"

She moves to the back of the car and snaps open the latches on two black cases, checking her inventory. Gloves. Coveralls. Respirators. Boot covers. A few test tubes and indicators for basic chemical typing. Her ultrasonic beam. The nanobots. Her better computer is back at the office, but she can couple most of her instrumentation to her phone and transmit the data to the nearest satellite.

She taps the third case, the metal one. She can't open that here—doesn't want to ever open it, honestly. But the solid thud tells her the case is full and ready to go if worse comes to worst.

"I think I have everything. If I drive, can you encrypt my phone? I'm going to need to send some heavy data pretty far."

William gets out of the driver's seat and walks around the back of the car, stealing a quick kiss as they pass. "Absolutely. I already mapped the location." They both get in and reflexively checked to see if they have been followed. It seems clear.

"Did you talk to Deerdra this morning? She seemed…odd."

"I noticed that, too. We'll talk to her tonight. But right now, make sure that signal's secure and tell me what happened."

The car slips out into traffic and speeds out toward farm country.

Chapter 15
Dressed for Spying

Barb and Gavin sit side by side on the front steps. Today, Barb is dressed for spying—black turtleneck, olive drab camouflage cargo pants, and black sneakers. Her hair is in a sleek bun, and she's wearing dark sunglasses. She's sketching something on a notebook, talking to Gavin and pointing here, then there, sliding her finger around and flipping between pages.

Gavin is Gavin. Jeans and a hoodie and a gentle smile on his face. He closes his eyes and leans his head back, processing Barb's chatter and the sunshine and whatever thoughts are in his own head. If Barb is energy, Gavin is gravity. He's just so solid, somehow.

"The eagle has landed!" Barb pats the stair next to her, and I sit. "Zhu scrahbbed zee mishhun, comrade. Vhat hyappened?"

"Mr. Jerkhin happened. He saw me walking, and he pulled over and yelled at me. He said he knew what we were up to. And I think he was drunk? He was definitely angry." I half close one eye, point a clawed hand, and try a wheezing breath. "'I. Know. What. You're. Doing.' That kind of thing?"

Barb and Gavin stare for a split second, both break up laughing.

"Not bad," Gavin says.

"It just seemed like a bad time to be holding on to any evidence," I say.

"Aw, pumpkin, you really are new," said Barb, patting my head. "Mr. Jerkhin was DEFINITELY drunk. Did you know he started as a science teacher? He was, like, smart and nerd-cute and interesting. My oldest sister had him and loved him. You could ask anything science-y, and he'd talk about it for the entire period, but he kept it interesting. A Lupin, not a Binns, you know? After a couple of years, he started to fall apart. Some days were fine, and other days, he'd ramble and get mad. On the worst days, he didn't even shower—he'd just stink and slur his words and get angry at everyone. One day he was prepping for a chem lab, and something went wrong and he blew off a finger. My sister said the school saved like a million dollars by letting him stay on and work as a janitor instead of firing him. Lawsuit city."

"Really?"

"Yep! Look at his right hand next time you see him—he's missing part of his middle finger."

"Like Jerry Garcia!" One of my favorite Earth singers lost half a finger on his right hand in a wood-chopping incident when he was a child.

"Um…" Barb says.

"The Grateful Dead!" I say. On the ship, Mother and I spent some time researching this part of American Earth culture. There's nothing like it in Anthean culture. They started as a "jug band" in San Francisco. They played at something called the "acid tests" before LSD, a rudimentary psychedelic not unlike G223, which we use for training of domestic animals. They somehow managed to maintain their audience for decades and decades, through many keyboard players and ups and downs and finally even through the death of founding member and icon Jerry Garcia. I know so much about the Grateful Dead, and I'm sure Gavin and Barb know even more—after all, they grew up here. We can connect over the Dead and elevate our relationship to at least a strong secondary. Maybe even roll it over to primary.

"Who?"

Oh.

"You know them, Barb. My mom played Touch of Grey all last summer when things were bad with my dad." He taps a beat on her knee while he half sings "I willlll…get byyyyy-yyyyy-yyy…I will surviiiive…"

"Ohhhhh! And she used to play their live stuff when we were little kids! I remember that—the parents would have some wine, and we'd spin around in your backyard for a while, and then we'd go do whatever while they argued about B-sides. Deerdra, you would have loved this dress I had then; it was really long, and I'd twirl around and—"

"Hold up, Barb." Gavin's spine straightens, and he adjusts his glasses. "That's a really good point."

"What's a good point? Our parents used to get buzzed when they were supervising young children, and you and I could do whatever we wanted for an hour or so while they sobered up?"

"Pretty much. Deerdra says Jerkhin had a big liquid breakfast. Want to go get that file back while he's sleeping it off?"

Barb grins. "Hell yeah. Deerdra, you in?"

Even if this weren't my mission, I'd do it. Just to try to keep Barb and Gavin smiling at me like they are now. "Of course."

Barb flips through the notebook where she's drawn at least a dozen diagrams of the school. Hallways with major landmarks. Classrooms with each teacher's name written in calligraphy above the door. Some of the maps are more detailed than my own. She must have stayed up until midnight working on them. She walks her fingers through the to-scale hallways as she talks. "I think we need a three-pronged plan of attack. I'll pretend that I hurt my ankle and head to the nurse. Then she'll get me some crutches from the equipment room, and Gavin can distract her by faking the stomach flu just outside, and Deerdra can sneak in and grab the playbook. Obviously, I'll have to change shoes because these are too sturdy. There's no way I'd roll an ankle in them. So first, we're going to have to break into the costume room off of the theater. That'll take about ten minutes. Gavin, can you puke on command, or do we have to mix up something in the cafeteria to fake it?"

"Barb. *Generalissimo.*" He gives a small salute. "This is a very good plan, but the bell rings in ten minutes. What if you sneak into the storage room and get the file, and Deerdra and I will stand at either end of the hall and text you if it's not safe to come out?"

Barb and Gavin. Energy and gravity. I had no idea that humans would be so different, or that their differences would make them so special to me. I pull out my cell phone.

"I have Barb's number, but I need Gavin's. I'm ready if you are."

Chapter 16
William and Stefanie: Are We Alone?

The drive is quite pleasant, if they don't think too much about what's waiting for them. This area of the country is lovely—rolling fields and red barns and livestock. Every curve brings something new. When they first landed, they archived their cultural study materials and spent a few weeks doing reconnaissance around the country, testing their new identities and monitoring the chatter on the military channels whenever they'd appear or disappear on the radar. It was important to gauge the reactions on a micro level, so they could extrapolate what may happen if more than one ship arrived, more than one small family of three.

They sent the Colonel the analysis of their bodies' reactions to lighter Earth gravity, but they didn't mention how much they laughed that day in the desert, where their naturally stronger muscles turned them into the superheroes that they'd seen in movies, leaping over cacti that were almost a story tall. At night, they sat on the sun-warm rocks and finalized the human names they would use, practicing their introductions with their favorite candidates.

They were surely the Greys, thanks to a nickname Stefanie's father acquired during his first mission. It was as close as they'd come to a family name.

Deerdra was Deerdra almost right away, although she was very nearly a Killian. Mother wasn't quite a Sheila or an Erin. Maybe a Tara? No, nothing felt quite as right as Stefanie. Father had the hardest time choosing a name. "It is nice to meet you. I am Joe. I am new." Not quite right. "I am Michael?" No. Dan? Tony? Matthew? Chris? Tom?

Eventually, he was William. "Bill, to my friends," he said, staring at his slightly doughy cheeks in the mirror as he extended his hand. "I am new. I am very happy to make your acquaintance."

After they had names, William and Stefanie and Deerdra would go to the beach and stare in wonder at the water that stretched as far as their eyes could see. All of that not-yet-ruined water, warmer than it should be, yes, but not yet at a tipping point, not quite. Their own oceans were dead, roiled with the bodies of the beings that had once called them home, fouled beyond leisurely use now. It was the cost of being an advanced society. They had all learned this simple fact in school. The oceans and the rivers and the skies and plants were a small price to pay for the benefits of advancement. Not every society had a seat at the Council.

They watched the Earth families as they played in the water. Played in the water! Without burning their skins, mutating their DNA, or wearing dry suits. It was amazing.

Humans were obviously less intelligent, but there was something charming about them. They were tribal, of course—each familial group tended to keep to itself although there was some mixing among the juveniles. The infants and toddlers would stay close to their familial units, but the older children would form swarms and run up and down the beach. The teenagers were the outliers, sometimes staying with their families and ignoring them, then sneaking off to practice mating rituals on the boardwalk or under the pier. The social lines weren't as clear-cut as some of the movies would indicate. It's hard to differentiate Nerds from Populars when everyone is wearing similar bathing suits and eating damp, gritty sandwiches out of insulated cooler bags.

As researchers, it was interesting to see their subjects go from theoretical case studies to living, breathing beings on the same beach. They'd occasionally even let Deerdra play with some of the older children. It was a rare opportunity for a young researcher to really interact with her subject matter. And it made for some excellent photos to send back to Anthea. Stefanie wanted to use the photo of Deerdra sharing a huge tub of popcorn with several humans as the cover of their holiday report.

Those first few weeks on Earth, when exploration was just for their own personal pleasure and not about their mission, were some of the best.

But now it was the mission, the highway and the cornfields rolling yellow on either side of the sedan, William with his foot on the pedal and Stefanie taking readings as they progressed.

"We should really take a weekend off sometime," William says, trying to break the tense silence. Trying to pretend this is just another drive. "Get in the car and drive somewhere new. We could do a long weekend at Mammoth Cave. Deerdra's probably tired of the humans at her school, and I'm sure we could convince the General that we need to know about the subterranean environment here. If, for example, our people couldn't handle too much time in the sun, or need a way to hide from the Reptilians…"

Stefanie smiles sadly at her husband. "If there are Reptilians to hide from, it'll already be too late."

William fiddles with the dials on the console. He turns on the heat and opens the tanks of synthetic atmosphere, morphing the vehicle into a miniature version of their regeneration chamber. He inhales deeply and feels his brain and body re-energize a bit as the chemicals work through the layers of his biosuit. Depending on how these field tests go, they could be in for a long night.

He twists another knob. As much as he has tried, as much as he studied the theory and history of the genre and its socioeconomic and historical impacts, he just doesn't like country music.

Chapter 17
Super Spies

Gavin was right, of course—the simplest solution is the best solution. The halls are always chaotic before first period, flooded with overachievers leaving their morning club meetings, late drop-offs rushing out of their parents' cars, couples trying to squeeze in a few more minutes of handholding and light making out before the bell separates them. Barb slipped into the storage room and back to the hallway in less than a minute, looking mildly disappointed and carrying another folder stuffed full of paper.

"Nothing? Just in and out? I don't get to do a barrel roll or work on my accents or match wits with a strong, handsome counter-agent?"

Gavin nods down the hall toward the supply and mechanical room. "Mr. Jerkhin's probably napping down there. We could wake him up. There's probably some good muscle under that flannel. He'd be like the paper-towel guy..."

"I hate you."

"I know. You couldn't love me as much as you do if you didn't hate me a little."

Barb kisses him on the tip of his nose. I feel a quick fast version of the itch under my skin that I felt at breakfast. I am...annoyed? No, not quite.

I think this is jealousy.

Not much. I like both of them immensely, but I wish I could be that close to someone. Barb and Gavin understand each other—like each other without an obvious benefit. They're not dating, so they're not receiving any of the immediate or long-term advantages of procreation. Their bond alienates them from the rest of the students, so they're not gaining any standing within their community.

They just really like each other. The benefit of their relationship is their relationship.

Then Gavin reaches out and grabs her hand, and then grabs my hand, and the itch goes away. The warmth of his fingers should stay localized in the palms of my biosuit, but I swear I can feel heat travel through my fingers, up my arm, and up until my heart squeezes, squeezes in my chest.

"Mission accomplished, super spies."

I try to speak confidently, but all I can do is squeak out, "Mmhmm."

Barb grabs Gavin by the back pocket, spins him around, and slides the thick folder into his backpack.

"Can you hold on to this, Gav?" She's already zipping the pack back up. "Deerdra and I are going to be the primary suspects. Provided Jerkhin can remember anything from yesterday. Big 'if,' of course, but better to be safe."

"Sure. Good call."

Barb air-kisses at both of us and whispers, "Lyater, cohmrades!" The she flattens herself against a locker, looks both ways, performs a spin move, grabs a ninth-grader, and leads him in a few confused tango steps around a corner. The girl knows how to make an exit.

Gavin extends an elbow like a gentleman in an old movie. "I can't top that, so: may I escort you to the land of pure imaginary numbers?"

"But of course!"

We walk arm in arm down the hall.

Chapter 18
William and Stefanie and the Bad News

The black sedan pulls over on the shoulder by a wheatfield. William takes one more big lungful of regenerative gas before he steps out of the car. He hopes this is a waste of a morning. He hopes he can spend an hour in this field, watching his wife search for evidence that doesn't exist. She'll go through all of the diagnostic tests in the first black case, and then the second, and the reagents will stay the same color and the instrument's clicks will only give the low-level purr indicating standard background radiation. He'll go back to the office and drink coffee—coffee has been a pleasant culinary surprise on this planet—and lightly complain to Tim From Work with Glasses about all of the things that he could have accomplished today. He hopes Ted from Accounting hasn't already claimed the yellow cup with "Big Hug Mug" written on it in big red letters from the shared dinnerware in the kitchenette. William has grown fond of the Big Hug Mug. Maybe that will be the biggest disappointment of the day—being stuck with the mug emblazoned with the Monday-hating pasta feline.

But no. They can already see the crop circle. The crushed wheat forms spiraling arms that stretch out over an acre. Spiraling arms that, if you know your astronomy, match a certain galaxy about 587 light years away. Their home galaxy, in fact.

"Stefanie…" he murmurs. He doesn't know what to say next.

"I know. I see it, too. The best thing we can do for them now is to get them data, and fast."

They take measurements. Stefanie's dedication to accuracy is the right scientific choice, but it feels excruciatingly slow to the mission commander. He keeps hoping for a negative test. Something to show that this is a bored human with two-by-four on a string, or a false flag from the government, or ball lightning.

But no. Every answer aligns with what they already know. They upload the results to a phone, take photos, and beam it all up into space. General Primicerius will see the reports in a week. By then it might be too late.

The Reptilians are already here.

Chapter 19
Mrs. V is in the House

I almost don't notice the signal. The Colonel recommends we listen to local radio, and a song has gotten stuck in my head, an older one, something Gavin calls "hair metal." *Round and Round...with love, we'll find a way—just give it time...round and round...* It's the most stupid thing I've ever heard, repetitive and insulting, and either I'm missing something or the words do not actually assemble into a meaningful narrative. The singer cannot sing. And yet, there it is, stuck in my head, again and again and round and round, for nearly my entire walk home.

I wonder if this is a permanent situation. Could this be related to my mission? Perhaps Eunice found herself in a similar position and simply couldn't go on living with some annoying song snippet replaying itself endlessly in her thoughts. Perhaps when we take over this planet, we will rid the world of all copies of this song. Perhaps we'll make it our new anthem.

Another day, some other way... We're gonna go, but then we'll see you again... I've had enough, we've had enough...

In this daze, I almost don't notice the planter, the way it has been pushed to the very front of the porch. It's a sign. Trouble.

I pause on the porch to get my communication device ready, and I can hear voices, high-pitched and loud and...laughing?

I step in the door cautiously and listen.

"Suuuuuch a lovely kitchen," a strange voice says. It's bright and insistent. It could be a voice-over on the commercials that play during Mother's house-buying shows. This is a voice stuffed full of blenders and sundresses, ranch dressing and dishwashing detergent and apple-scented hair conditioner.

"Juuuuust lovely!" the voice blares. The edge of critique is unmistakable.

"Thank youuuuu," Mother says. "Thank you very muuuuuch." She's trying to match the intensity, the sheer brightness of the other voice, but I can tell she's scared. There is protocol here that she doesn't understand. If I can hear this, I'm sure the other woman can as well.

I enter the kitchen and can see the relief in Mother's eyes.

"And this MUST be Deerdra!" A woman, who does indeed look like she walked off the house-buying shows, approaches me with her arms outstretched. I engage my hand at forty-five degrees, make eye contact, and prepare for a traditional greeting, but before I know it, I'm enveloped in those arms. She squeezes tight, and my mouth is pushed up against her hair and I smell apples and perfume and money. She's wiry and stronger than she looks. She pulls back, grips my hands, and spreads my arms wide. She regards me as if she's just stumbled upon the most magical surprise.

"Aren't you just lovely?" she says. I stand there and feel more alien than ever. My bra is cutting into my side, and my feet feel gigantic. The waistband of my jeans is pushing at my belly. "Isn't she just a princess?" the woman says. She scans down my chest and stomach and hips, like the skunk in the cartoons. "And such a figure!"

I do not feel lovely. I do not feel like a princess. "Slightly above average," I say.

"Nonsense, honey. Now, I am Mrs. Vance," she says. "But you can call me Mrs. V!" She nearly whispers the last part, like she's offering me an amazing gift, something not usually available to normal people.

"Thank you," I say. "Thank you, Mrs. V."

Mother opens the refrigerator. The adult tertiary friendship protocol says that a traditional welcome gesture for a guest in your home is the offering of a liquid beverage: a glass of water, or juice, or an alcoholic drink. Mother rummages in the refrigerator while Mrs. V and I smile at one another. Her teeth are white and straight, and her hair is golden and shiny, cut in a bowl around her neck. Her skin is also gold, tanned, and pulled tight over her face. She looks very much like the women in the Real Housewives documentaries.

"Oh, here we go. Wine is necessary with everything the politicians are doing nowadays. And the weather! At least we have the Colts," Mother says. She hands Mrs. V a bottle of white wine from the refrigerator.

Mrs. V smiles even brighter. "Oh my," she says. "You folks from New Mexico must start earlier than we do here in the Midwest. And on a Tuesday, no less! We tend to make our own fun, you know, but different strokes, I suppose! I can make an exception if that's what you're used to."

I'm scanning my brain to remember the wine protocols. I haven't been briefed in this arena. I'm not old enough here to drink this beverage.

"Are you still getting unpacked?" Mrs. V says. She's looking at the drawers. She taps a shiny, pointed fingernail on the top of the bottle. I remember this now. These bottles sometimes must be opened by an archaic device called a wine opener.

Their language is so silly. Of course, the wine must be opened by something called a wine opener.

Mother is blank-faced. She tried three standard conversation starters, and Mrs. V didn't take to any of them. I can see sparks of panic flaming in her eyes.

This worries me more than anything. Mother is unflappable. She could have been our Mission Leader but declined the job so she could serve as Chief Science Officer. She once fixed a faulty photon shield on the outside of our ship as we were hurtling toward the wormhole that would jump us from Cygnus into the Milky Way. She could have been bombarded by a lethal dose of radiation or sucked out into the vacuum of deep space. After, when the shields were repaired and we were safely through the ten-second jump and another 100 light years closer to Earth, I asked her if she was scared. She simply blinked and said, "Fear wasn't a productive choice."

"Welcome to our home," she says now. She looks at the bottle in Mrs. V's hands and nods as if the transaction has been completed. "Now I really must attend to my family meal that is approaching. It is Taco Tuesday." She looks at the stove as if this explains everything.

Mrs. V nods and smiles but some of the light has gone out of her eyes. "Right," she says. "Terrific. Just great. Well, thank you. I'll leave this here in case you need it." She holds up the bottle and places it back on the counter. "It's just been real interesting to meet you," she says.

She walks past me and runs her hand down a lock of my hair, resting her hand briefly on my neck. "It is just like cornsilk, dear! Usually, brunettes don't get so lucky with texture. Mmm! Catch you girls later!" And she walks out, and the door clicks shut.

Mother and I stand and look at each other, enveloped in a nebula of perfume. "I…I do not know how to categorize her," says Mother. "Are there Real Housewives in Indiana?"

"Not that I know of." I hitch my backpack back up on my shoulder, feeling the weight of the Eunice Tiffany file. I need time to study it on my own, so I use the cover story I developed on my walk home, amidst the *round and round.* "I have a lot of homework tonight, Mother. A creative writing paper. The assignment our system generated only got a C, and I'd like to try writing something myself this time. If I get a better grade, we could report back to the Colonel and suggest some upgrades for the algorithm. Fiction writing is so pointless, but I guess it keeps the humans occupied."

"Yes. It's good of you to think of the mission," sighs Mother. "Actually, I need to work on a report myself. Your father and I did fieldwork in an actual field today. All very boring, of course, but I should file my paperwork. Shall we skip dinner tonight and spend a little extra time in the regeneration chamber? It would be more efficient." She shoots me a conspiratorial smile. "Why we…we could have tacos on *Wednesday*!" And then quickly, guiltily, "No. The paperwork involved would be astronomical."

"Of course. Well, I should write that paper." I smile with my biosuit mouth, happy for once that my real face is hidden. I have never lied to my mother before. I pick up my backpack and head to my room. Just before I close my door, I hear a throaty pop—Mother must have figured out how to uncork the wine.

Funny. Why would she want a drink after a day of field work?

PRELIMINARY FINDINGS:
EUNICE TIFFANY INVESTIGATION RECORDS

From: Terranaut 6.54.C, Outpost 3429-E, Orion-Cygnus Arm
To: Colonel Muckinzee, Outpost NGC-6946, Fireworks Galaxy

OVERVIEW:

With the aid of two human associates, I obtained Eunice Tiffany's school and police records. Following Level 4 Security Protocol, I transmitted an encrypted copy of her file. I will send the encryption key via a separate channel after 24 hours.

The file is a compilation of interviews with school staff and students, her academic and personal records, and occasional external input.

HABITS:

Agent Tiffany was in a number of school clubs. She was a leader in the Future Farmers of America, the drama club, and the Green Team. Her guidance counseling records suggest future careers in agribusiness, supply chain management, astronomy, or systems engineering.

Despite her friendly nature while at school, Agent Tiffany spent much of her time alone. She was often seen riding her bike, and later driving her car around the county. The police record reports a local fisherman saw her on her bike at sunrise, nearly 20 miles outside of town, saying:

> "Usually the only ones up at dawn on a Tuesday are me and the mosquitoes. I was surprised to see this young lady out for a bike ride. What kind of girl goes for a ride, alone, at 4 a.m.? Especially with such a heavy backpack?"

KNOWN ASSOCIATES:

There are two people referred to in the police report as *Individual A* and *Individual B*. *Individual A* is a known associate of Agent Tiffany's. *Individual B* was a suspect who had an alibi although the reporting officer notes some feelings of suspicion.

Names are redacted, but given the data, *Individual A* is Kayla Winchester, the Alpha Popular. *Individual B* is Michael Jerkhin, a school custodian.

FAMILY:

This section of the police report has been entirely redacted, on the orders of T. Lincoln Martinez, Director of the NSA.

DISAPPEARANCE:

This section of the police report has been moderately redacted, on the orders of T. Lincoln Martinez, Director of the NSA. The cause of the fire was never revealed. Agent Tiffany was identified via medical records—her dental evidence had been dropped—and local authorities appear satisfied with this result.

Local newspaper accounts detail a fire at a dairy, with follow-up investigation being taken over by the FBI due to the possibility of contaminated dairy cultures.

This is where, as you are well aware, Earth investigations leave off and our own inquiries take over.

Chapter 20
Can I Trust Anyone?

I hit SEND on the report and rub my eyes. My summary of the investigation may be read by Colonel Muckinzee, General Primicerius, and even their superiors. If they choose to read the files themselves, they'll see a thorough report.

What they won't see, however, is what I've learned by combining the files with several months of living Eunice's life—living in Danaville, going to Danaville High, talking and listening every day. I don't know what to do with this information. I don't know who I can trust.

Eunice and I could have been friends. If she'd even be my friend. She was given advantages that I was not. The reports constantly reference her looks, her brains, her beautiful singing voice. The inventory from her abandoned locker was a long list of luxury brands. Why did the General design Eunice's cover to be a Popular, and design my cover to be…me?

I know I should be happy for the slightly-above-average advantages I have, but it would have been easier to be Eunice.

Still, the reports show that Eunice's life and my life are variations on a theme, the mashed-up beats of a few familiar songs. Eunice was interested in agriculture? So is my mother. She spent her off-hours visiting the creek, the forest, and the farms in the area? So does my father. Every day, in between bites of oatmeal, Father tells about the day ahead, or little details from the day before. How he observed the livestock at the Redeker farm without being detected. The algebraic curves of the dragonflies dancing around a creek.

Why are Mother and Father picking up her research? Who is Eunice Tiffany? And more importantly, why don't we know what happened to her? My pre-mission briefings always stopped at the disappearance. No details about the investigation, no interviews with her parents. Why did my superiors load me up with pop culture factoids but never told me anything about the girl who is supposed to be my mission?

Even so, I've figured out a few things on my own.

Mr. Jerkhin—Individual B—was more than just an advisor to Kayla, but I don't know what their relationship was. If he was an official mission contact, she would have included him in her reports, but she never mentions him. Well, the files I received from the General never mention him.

I found Mr. Jerkhin in nearly a decade's worth of yearbooks. Barb's sister was right—ten years ago, Mr. Jerkhin looked like an actor in a movie about a science teacher. He's in the center of the photo, smiling up from a chair. He holds a plant in his lap, and several students behind him rest their hands on his shoulders. Black, horn-rimmed glasses enhance his bright eyes and square jaw. He's in a trim-fit tweed jacket with elbow patches. Not a short, shiny hair out of place.

Mr. Jerkhin was, at one time, far above average.

No.

Mr. Jerkhin was hot.

But he quickly devolves—the next year, the jacket's gone, replaced by a wrinkled polo. His face is a bit puffy. The year after, the tape on the bridge of his glasses emphasizes the new crow's feet around his dimmed eyes, and he's moved to the back row. By year six, he's in a corner, bushy hair obscuring the name embroidered on his coveralls, resting a hand on the potted plant that's jammed between him and the Green Team students—a four-fingered hand, the middle one lopped off at the middle joint. Just like Jerry Garcia.

Eunice shows up in the next year's Green Team photo. Mr. Jerkhin's there, too, slumped in a chair, jaundiced skin sagging like a candle left on a hot shelf. Eunice was just beginning her mission. She's been on Earth for about three months and has been a Danaville Fox for six weeks. A well-trained terranaut, she's shifted 70 percent of her weight to one side and crossed her arms, as the protocol manual dictates for a casual group photo among tertiary-level friends. But she's squinting a bit, and her left hand is blurry. The camera may have caught her when some new sensation overwhelmed her and she had to readjust the sensors on her biosuit. She is the most beautiful person in the photo, and her shoes alone cost more than my entire first week's wardrobe. I need to ask the Colonel why Eunice joined the Green Team. Was it to mimic Popular Kayla, who's standing in the middle of the photo, holding a potted American chestnut seedling, surrounded by friends? Or was it a matter of survival? If her biosuit was malfunctioning, the greenhouse could have served as a makeshift regeneration room—heat, sunlight, moisture, and carbon dioxide exhaled by the team members.

And finally, last year's photo. The front row, arm in arm: Kayla, Eunice, a now-thriving American chestnut sapling that seems to be wearing a taped-up pair of glasses, and Mr. Jerkhin. (Eunice flashes a peace sign. Kayla's caught mid-laugh, her face glowing. Mr. Jerkhin has swapped the coveralls for wrinkled Dockers, and a small, shy smile is back after a five-yearbook hiatus.)

The smile and the khakis, tiny steps of self-improvement. After Eunice disappeared, he dropped out of the Green Team and fell apart entirely.

The police records concluded that there was nothing inappropriate about their relationship. But as Barb pointed out, we have all seen enough crime procedurals to understand that when the pretty girl who is friendly with the weird janitor goes missing…well, the pretty girl just isn't friends with the weird janitor, to begin with, so where does that leave us? Did Mr. Jerkhin kill her? Is she being held captive in his basement? Was she his secret girlfriend? Or was he just a friend and advisor, somebody who's grieving and confused in the same way Kayla is grieving and confused?

I've learned more about Eunice through yearbook photos and Barb's stolen report than I ever did in my mission briefings from Father or the Colonel. If Eunice was so important, why don't I know anything about her other than "missing?" Why did someone so superior have to befriend an Earth girl and a janitor? Was that part of her mission, or just part of her personality? Actually, what was her mission? Was she here? And why is she gone?

What do Mother and Father know? Can I trust them?

Can I trust anyone?

Chapter 21
William's Long Day

William Grey is having a hard day at the office.

Finding evidence of Reptilians on Earth wasn't a shock. After all, the Reptilians were why most of the other Council planets achieved interstellar travel. In his grandfather's grandfather's time, Anthean astronomers confirmed that there was life on other planets. Soon after that, they realized that not all life on other planets was benevolent. They watched the Reptilians overthrow Kanigulus 22 with surprising speed and no apparent reservations. It was simple: a virus, created in a Reptilian lab, dropped from the sky. The Kaniguli, peaceful and simple, like upright Earth giraffes with more useful hand structures, were alive one day and dead the next. All of them. The Reptilian virus sped up decomposition, replenishing the soil and, in a master stroke of biological engineering, laid the eggs of the new master species. Long-necks out, lizards in.

Of course, there was an outcry from all other advanced civilizations. Like a dozen other planets in the nearby galaxies, Anthea's scientists refurbished their lunar rovers and their interplanetary cruisers and developed interstellar travel.

It was ugly and messy, and every planet had a wall, or a garden, or a statue somewhere commemorating the lives that were lost—frozen in the absolute zero of space, ripped apart by G-forces, broiled by radiation when their shields failed. And then there were the Makkel, who just forgot to pack food. Every one of their mission crew assumed food was on someone else's checklist—it had to be, who would be stupid enough to forget food? ("An easy mistake," said every diplomat in the Council, clucking their tongues and rasping their mandibles and outputting sympathetic waves of ultraviolet light. "For those idiots," they mumble-rasp-outputted when the translators were off and the ethanol infusers had made a few rounds.)

The uprising was inferior to the Reptilian's technology, but they saw a headache in the making. Why spend all of your time building walls and expending resources when your new enemies are going to join together to build better and better ladders and dig deeper tunnels? So much easier to befriend than fight. And so, the Council of Advanced Civilizations was formed.

On his cynical days, William believes the Council to be nothing more than a proxy organization for the Reptilians themselves, a body that doesn't so much regulate as facilitate the Reptilian agenda. On his less cynical days, he tries not to think about it at all.

"Ouch!" William's scalpel slips and slashes a small cut in his finger. The fact that it hurts is actually quite impressive—the neural network on his biosuit received the damage, interpreted it as pain, and delivered a shock to his actual nervous system in the appropriate place. *Science is a marvel,* he thinks. The one true religion.

The cut is deep, and William can see his actual finger for the first time in months. It's small and grey and totally smooth. Funny how his real fingers seem too long and skinny now, reaching out like leafless tree branches. Irritated with his clumsy knife work and his wandering mind, William roots through a nearby first aid kit and applies a serum to the cut surface. That will hold the biosuit together well enough for now, and he'll bump up the regeneration cells in the car on the drive home. Crank them up to eleven.

Along with the radio. What a day.

Earth still has some time. The Reptilians can adapt to any planet, but they need a tremendous amount of environmental data to do so. Soil composition. Atmospheric makeup. The cell structure of plants. Their advance teams take thousands of samples, maybe millions, and send the data to their incubation ships. Fertilization technicians stick the eggs in a nutrient bath, calibrated to the new environment, and then hide clutches of eggs around the new planet. In a few months, the new Reptilians hatch, fully adapted and ready to infiltrate.

As a scientist, William sort of admires the crop circles. They're the aftereffects of the Reptilians' agricultural studies. If there were a way that he could walk away from his current lab work—a specimen dissection that's proving to be messier than average—and know that if anyone stumbled on it, it would be considered mysterious mathematical art, he'd do it. Clean-up is messy, but damage control is messier.

But that's the other purpose of the crop circles—how do the dominant species on the planet react? If they don't react at all, the Reptilians know it will be an easy takeover. They'll establish a new colony, but only eliminate the populace if and when it's necessary. If there is a coordinated military response—which almost never happens, especially when most species are engaged in ridiculous wars among themselves over arbitrary terrestrial borders—then the Reptilians opt for world domination. The ship descends, they drop a virus, cough cough cough, and the planet is theirs in a few weeks. Nobody left to fight back. The dust settles, the eggs hatch, and the Reptilians rule another planet.

William hates these brute-force attacks. Where is the artistry? Why bother learning about a planet only to obliterate it? Is the point of becoming an advanced society simply to trample the less evolved? Perhaps. Perhaps not. Who is he to even be thinking these thoughts? Right now, the job is clear. The Reptilians were running an unsanctioned mission, and they don't have the proper permits from the rest of the Council.

He checks his texts—a few from Stefanie, who's reviewing their interstellar transmitter arrays and their weapons cache. After they're secured, she'll alert the other Earthbound non-Reptilian Council members about their findings. He has a few hours to finish this study and get anatomy logged before things go into crisis mode. He re-gloves and starts the delicate work of ocular dissection.

There are a number of things William doesn't like about their current mission. Their chain of command is too complex, and it takes too long to make decisions. It takes a week to get a communique to Anthea, another week for the response to come back. And who knows how long it will take Home Command to actually make a decision? But the chain is thorough. They have the proper permits.

Antheans are slowly colonizing Earth, hidden in biosuits. Some focus on research, while others infiltrate governments and media empires. They have had a decent success rate so far. Tim from Work with Glasses is their highest-placed agent and is continuing the outreach program that Stefanie's father pioneered long ago, after the first crash.

They'll make things more amenable for the Antheans, then the big reveal. General Primicerius' obsession with Earth pop culture isn't just for his own entertainment. They've created countless hours of programming to introduce the idea of other life forms, even repackaging actual events as fiction. How can you fear aliens when you've binge-watched eighteen hours of doe-eyed aliens overthrowing evil human governments and saving the day? Aliens like waffles and peanut butter candies. Aliens have magical connections with wildlife and respect the Earth environment more than humans themselves. Aliens have long, flowing hair and big, rippling biceps and use their superhuman strength for good. Aliens: they're just like us!

Eventually, fiction will become fact, and the humans' response will determine their fate. If there is an uprising, it will be dealt with. William doubts it will be a problem. Humans have a strong herd mentality and like to stay comfortable.

SPLORCH. Damn this Earth gravity. So easy to forget you're more powerful than the objects around you. He should clean up and go home. Too many things to do.

"And I'm not going to get any real research done today," he murmurs to the lifeless form on his operating table. "Look at this—I've absolutely mutilated this cow."

Chapter 22
Green Team

Joining the Green Team is the most logical next step for my investigations, both official and unofficial. I convinced Barb to come with me, and she's farmer-chic today: overalls, vintage Farm Aid shirt, and a red bandana kerchief framing two braids. Barb plays with the ends while we sit on the south lawn and get a pep talk from the advisor who replaced Mr. Jerkhin.

Coach K's approach to Green Team is more physical than environmental. He paces in front of us like a panther, smacking a clipboard for emphasis as he talks. "Be the change you want to see, children. We could talk about the impacts"—*slap!*—"of global warming, or we could get OUT there!" *Slap SLAP slap!* "Roll UP our sleeves!" *Slap SLAP slap slap.* "Plant some plants!" *Slap slap slap.* "Encourage people to walk!" He gently spikes the clipboard to the ground.

He continues, shoving his sunglasses up the bridge of his nose with one finger. "Now it's game weekend, and there are a number of sad-looking flower beds near the football booster parking area. The only thing sadder than a sad-looking flower is a sad-looking football booster. Now let's get out there, Green Team, grab some compost, and MULCH! Do it for the planet! AND DO IT FOR THE FOXES!"

Barb swings her head around at me, her face deadpan. "We're going to mulch on our lunch break? Deerdra, I believe that charismatic sports gentleman is full of compost."

I toss a bag of compost into a wheelbarrow. "Think of the generations of intrepid mulchers who came before you, Barb! Their primitive mulching technology." This is straight out of the General's mission launch speech. "Those brave gardeners wouldn't even dream of touching the edges of the fabric of the overflow parking lot. It's come to this. It's up to us." I hand her a pitchfork. She grabs it and salutes, then leaves her hand in place and curls back all but her middle finger.

"BARBARA! Not on my watch." Coach K shoots an eyebrow Barb's way. "Let's keep the filth with the flowers, now. Grey, wheelbarrow drill. Let's go let's go let's go!"

Coach K blows his whistle. Barb and I trundle off to the far parking lot. She plays around with the pitchfork while we walk. It's a bow staff, then it's a vaulting pole, then it's a cane in a soft-shoe dance. I wonder if Barb ever gets tired. I wonder if she's ever looked in a mirror and doubted who she is. How could she? She's whoever she wants to be.

We reach the far parking lot and start cleaning the beds and working the compost into the dirt. Orange marigolds and yellow daylilies dot the sunny spots, while waxy, green hostas and pink impatiens peek out from the shade. Not the showiest flowers, but all of them hardy. Picked to stand on their own and be neglected more than they'd be noticed. It feels good to give them some time and some nutrients.

Barb's filling me in on the latest gossip among the Danaville theater set—apparently, the drama on the stage is nothing compared to the drama behind the scenes, in the wings, and one memorable time on the bus to see a musical in Chicago—when she stiffens. "I forgot *she* was on Green Team."

I follow her gaze and see Kayla jogging over to Coach K. He hands her a watering can, says something I can't hear, and squeezes her shoulder. She half smiles, grabs the can, and puts on her sunglasses.

Barb wipes her hands on the grass and stands. "This has been swell, but I've had all of the manure that I can handle for one day. I'm going to go clean up." She walks stiffly away, arms folded. When she crosses Kayla's path, they both stare straight ahead, neither acknowledging the other's presence.

What's the proper protocol here? If I intend to move Barb from a secondary to primary friendship, I should follow her. Ask what happened with Kayla. Nod in affirmation at everything she says, regardless of the logic.

But if I want to advance my investigation… "Kayla. Hi. Um. Could you…could you water this flower bed? We ran out. I ran out. Well, Barb ran, and I am here, and I don't have enough water, and these marigolds will dry out."

Kayla's expression is frustratingly neutral, but she heads my way. In the distance, I see that Barb looks back, takes in the scene, and moves faster toward the school. I'll have to talk to her as soon as this is over.

Kayla tips water onto the plants, and I wrack my brain for an emergency conversational topic.

"Thanks. I didn't think to bring extra water with me. We didn't garden much in New Mexico."

Kayla's head snaps up. "Wait, you're from New Mexico? Where in New Mexico?"

"Santa Fe."

"Oh. How far is that from Roswell? I have…had…a friend from near there."

"Two hundred and fifty-eight miles." I remember taking the drive during our first few weeks here. Ten days in Santa Fe to learn enough about the city to develop our cover identities—I have memorized a dossier full of my "favorite" local restaurants, activities, and a few amusing anecdotes. Then we drove to Roswell, so Mother could see where her father landed in 1947. I remember standing outside the fence, Mother staring at the red desert sand. Later she went into a gift shop, emerging a minute later, pale and sweating, making Father pull the car over a few minutes later so she could vomit.

"That's…oddly specific." Kayla pushes her sunglasses up to the top of her head, holds one of the unplanted marigolds near her face, and snaps a few selfies.

"There was a road sign by our house with the mileage." I try to shake myself out of the memory. Find a new topic. Things within my line of sight? Marigold. There we go. "So, Kayla, why did you join the Green Team?"

She shrugs, "I mean, we only have the one planet, right?"

If only she knew. "Right."

"It's not like we can just fly off and take over Mars if we wreck this one, right?"

"Right." IF ONLY SHE KNEW. I need something to do with my hands, so I push my wheelbarrow over to the mulch pile and start loading. Kayla walks with me, plucking a few petals off of the marigold and rubbing them between her thumb and forefinger.

"So we need to do things sustainably, and plants are going to be a huge part of it." She extends her fingers, dyed like sunshine. "I want to start my own botanic makeup line someday. This cheapo marigold has antioxidants, is anti-fungal, antibacterial, and anti-inflammatory. And this orange is hot and would make the best eyeshadow."

Coach K blows his whistle. "Green Team! Pack it up and move out, double-time! The boosters and the planet appreciate what you've done today!"

Kayla sighs. "Man. I don't even know why I'm doing this. Coach K is no *Michael.*" She says the last word with a strong Southern accent.

"Michael?" I say it with the standard Midwestern accent, as per protocol.

"Mr. Jerkhin. He was the Green Team advisor until…until last year. You wouldn't know it to look at him, but he was actually pretty great? Anyway, he and a friend of mine had this running thing where he called her by her initials and she called him Michael. But always with that accent. *Mah-kul.* I have no idea why they got along so well—you've seen him—but it was fun. She made everything fun."

"Kayla? I'm sorry about Eunice. Everything I've heard about her…she sounded great." A very average statement about an exceptional girl. This is my life.

"She was. Hey. Um. I should apologize. About the shirt thing, from gym," Kayla says. "That shirt…it belonged to Eunice. Seeing it really messed me up, and there was no way you could have known about it."

"It's okay." Protocol dictates that this is the proper reply, but it feels so small. I want to tell Kayla that I know that she was Eunice's friend, and I want to learn everything about her friendship with Eunice, and I want to yell at her for being mad at me for something that I didn't know about. Couldn't have known about. Eunice's shirt was not regulation, after all.

"I can take this from here, ladies." Coach K walks over and takes the wheelbarrow from me. He grimaces when he lifts. "Grey, have you thought about powerlifting? How did you get this thing all the way back here? It must weigh two hundred pounds!"

I was so deep into my conversation with Kayla that I didn't think about the extra energy I was getting from the sun. I try to compensate, stretching my lower back and rubbing my palms with my thumbs as though they blistered from the heavy load. "Girl power, I guess?"

The warning bell rings, saving me from more discussion. Kayla glides away, back to the other Populars. I can feel our gossamer-thin connection stretching, know it's going to break again like a spiderweb. And then, she looks back and smiles. "Definitely not a *Michael.* But you have potential. See you in gym, Girl Power."

Chapter 23
Definitely Not a *Michael*

Kayla's words throb in my chest for the rest of the day. *"Definitely not a* Michael. *But you have potential."*

Potential to be a Popular? Potential to be Kayla's best friend, like Eunice before her?

For the rest of the afternoon, I pretend to take notes but instead make checklists and charts for my rise in Popularity. We'd say Father got a promotion and a raise. I could start wearing upscale labels and get a more stylish haircut. I could slowly drop the slightly-above-average cover identity altogether. Better grades, better at sports. That's easily explained away—I had an adjustment period after homeschooling, but now I'm acclimated to Danaville High and thriving. Then what? Cheerleader? School dances? Maybe a boyfriend?

I'll need a cover for the transformation. I'll have a cousin. A stylist in Philadelphia who engineers an entire makeover. Make it dramatic enough and I could even make a few tweaks to my biosuit. Take care of a few imperfections and get closer to above average. Maybe even exceptional. Maybe like Eunice.

The plan would take about four weeks to clear through our leadership. A long weekend for the redesign. I could start the process by Homecoming and be a full-on Popular by Christmas.

"Definitely not a Michael. *But you have potential."*

It's all for the mission, of course. I'll stay friends with Barb and Gavin, try to bring them into the Popular fold. They'd be good representatives for the rest of the student body—the best of the non-Populars. As a Popular, I'll have more activities and interactions with the rest of the student body. More opportunities to meet people without justification. I will be a Popular, and as a Popular, I'll be able to do whatever I want and talk to whoever I want without worrying about maintaining my slightly-above-average cover. Eunice could be friends with Mr. Jerkhin without damaging her reputation because she was already a Popular.

In fact, it may help the overall objective. If Kayla and I could be friends with Barb and Gavin, if Eunice could be friends with Mr. Jerkhin…with *Michael.* The Antheans could coexist with the humans, here on Earth. Humans coexist with cows. It would be like that. Like the Reptilians and the Makkel sitting together at the council. We could make it work.

I look out the window and see him outside, raking leaves. I wonder if we will be friends when I'm a Popular, or if he was only *Michael* to Eunice. I wonder if he'll start caring about his appearance again if Kayla and I include him in our Popular activities. He looks a mess now, standing in the courtyard and scratching the jaundiced skin on the nape of his neck.

And then, for just an instant, he slides his hand up through what looks like a long wrinkle on the back of his neck. A move I've done before when my biosuit felt constricting and I needed air on my skin.

Michael Jerkin.

Mah-kul Jerkin.

Makkel Jerkhin.

We're not alone in Danaville. And Eunice knew.

Chapter 24
Jerkhin

I review the files overnight, and it all lines up: Mr. Jerkhin is a Makkelian. Now that I know, I can't stop searching for him. I get to school early, leave late, hang around the halls as long as I can after the classroom bell. I see him from a distance, hurrying from one place to another, pushing his cleaning cart around, pulling his bucket and mop. He is large in every way—wide and tall and thick. He lurches. He sways. He is literally falling apart, collapsing into himself.

The Makkelians have clearly not been using the same slightly-above-average algorithm to calibrate their endoskeletons.

The idea that a Makkelian is here, in this Earth high school, some 300 light years from our homes, should completely freak me out. As Father said, they are an inferior species. But they—him, this hulking, poorly designed janitor who smells like medicine and breathes so loud you hear him snorting in his closet during lunch, who literally every single person in school seems terrified of, including the teachers and administration, who spends his days cleaning up puke and spills and sweeping floors—is also the closest I have to a peer in this school.

On Fridays after fifth period, I have a study hall that is monitored by the lacrosse coach, Mr. Robertson. I have attended this study hall every Friday, and I have yet to actually meet Mr. Robertson. I picture him as a blond, tall man twirling a netted stick in his large, gloved hands. In reality, Mr. Robertson is an empty chair, a missing space at the head of fifth-period study hall. I have heard whispers that he spends all his time in the basement doing something called "watching tape."

I have no idea how a grown man can watch a ring of adhesive for fifty minutes every Friday, but I take advantage of this situation by not reporting to study hall. First I wander the school, listening for his breathing, watching for the telltale snail trail of Jerkhin's mop. Nothing. I walk into the bathroom and stare at myself in the mirror. I wish my hair was different but cannot put into thought exactly what I wish for it other than "something more like Kayla's hair."

Then I get an idea. I walk to the office, and when Mrs. Queen asks if she can help me, I tell her that I'm terribly sorry but somebody has just evacuated the contents of their stomach in the south hallway.

"Oh goodness," she says. "What do you think we should do?"

I pause. I didn't expect this line of questioning. She's smiling, waiting for me to answer. Or I think she's waiting for me to answer. "Call Mr. Jerkhin?" I say. It comes out more like a question than a statement.

Now Mrs. Queen pauses. "You sure, dear?" she says. "Mr. Jerkhin?"

"Yes, I think so."

"Okay, sweetie," she says as if I've just made some kind of serious decision.

She hits a button, and I hear her voice come over the intercom: "Mr. Jerkhin, cleanup on south hall. Cleanup on south hall."

One of his eyes is cloudy and grey and the other is bright, clear blue. He's limping, dragging his left foot. The buggy parts of his endoskeleton are all on the left side. I wonder if there's an issue with the energy source, or the connection between his own nervous system and his biosuit, or whatever they use to camouflage his actual appearance.

I hide around the corner and wait.

He drags his feet and clomps his rolling mop bucket. Drag-clomp. Drag-clomp as he gets closer. Drag-clomp drag-clomp drag-clomp around the corner and heading toward the puddle. Drag-clomp and he's almost here.

"Mmmmmngh," he exhales, a sound like a monster or an animal from the television. "What the…" he says.

I suddenly realize I know nothing, really, about Makkelians. Are they stronger than we are? Can they even be reasoned with? I take the pencil out of my backpack and hold the sharpened end out like a stake, like I'm confronting a vampire.

I suck in some air to quiet the activity in my sympathetic nervous system and step out from around the corner.

His mop is in the water, and he's bending over to look at the orange juice, tracing a finger around the puddle. He stops, looks at me. "No chunks," he says. He moves the finger around again and stands up, wheezing. He smells worse up close, like cigarettes and the broom closet and a familiar smell of medicine. I think about the look on Father's face when he said the word Makkel: "*A lower species.*"

"There aren't," he wheezes. "Any chunks." He smells his finger and then sticks it in his mouth. "Orange juice," he says.

I wait for something else, but he just picks up the mop and methodically cleans up the mess. He wheezes steadily, a low "mmmmmgh" mixing with the swish of the mop. The industrial cleaner mixes with Jerkhin-smell. My mouth waters and my stomach churns.

He leans in closer to me. He is massive, and I find myself looking directly at his sagging chest. He sniffs me, and I try not to jump. I'm still holding the pencil. If he attacks, I'll aim for one of his eyes or his reproductive organs and hope that Makkelian anatomy roughly aligns with his biosuit. He sniffs again and then steps back. "That's what. I thought," he says. "We need to." Wheeze. "Talk." He swipes the mop around a few more times, and I follow him back to the janitor's closet.

"Where are you from?" he says, closing the door. The smell of the room is overwhelming. This behavior is certainly not normal for a high school junior. I make a mental note that the Populars must not see me exiting this room. Jerkhin sits down in the corner chair. "Mmmmmngh."

"New Mexico?" I say. "But like…like Eunice."

He doesn't offer a response, but his left arm falls off and flops around on the floor like a brook trout. He wheezes again: "Mmmmmrgh." Father wasn't wrong about their species, or at least their bioengineering. Jerkhin picks the arm up and stuffs it back into the socket, feeling around for a connection. Finally, something clicks, and he sits back down, the arm hanging loosely at his side.

"Don't…go…anywhere," he wheezes. He lurches into a back room, and I catch a glimpse of the warm grey glowing in the corners, feel soothing cool air. He has a regeneration chamber, too. I wait. The room makes a low hum.

He knew about Eunice. That much is clear. And he's not going to hurt me. Even if he tried, I don't know that he'd be able to do much.

There's a rustle in the back room, and the hum cuts out, and I realize how quiet it is, still between classes, the only sound the faint tinkle of silverware being sorted in the cafeteria's kitchen. The chamber opens, and he closes it carefully, taking his time with several locks. He looks better. Smells better. The skin on his face and neck have returned to a hue of yellow-pink that, while not looking actively healthy, at least conveys a lack of an active disease.

"Terribly sorry," he says. "But I believe. You understand."

I nod.

"Do you know where she is?" he says.

"Who?"

The loudspeaker. The principal's voice. "Mr. Jerkhin, please come to the office immediately. Thank you."

Jerkhin stands up. He gathers some things—rags and cleaners and a pencil, off the table.

"Eunice," he says. "Where's Eunice?"

My mind is swirling with options, none of which seem like the right thing. There's nothing in the manual for this. In the absence of a better idea, I tell him the truth: "I don't know. Why do you care? Why are you here?"

"Anthea isn't the only planet. In trouble. The Council sent me here. Too. We have much. To talk about," he says. His face is already starting to turn pale, and his left shoulder is already shrinking. He wheezes again. "I will find you. Soon." he says. "And we will talk."

He steps through the door, drag-clomp, and I'm alone in the room.

Chapter 25
Mrs. V is Back in the House

I hear her before I see her. Her laugh. It's Saturday, and I'm in my room, looking through magazines when I hear the broken-glass laugh tinkling up the stairs from the kitchen. Father says something, and there it is again, pushing up the stairs and boring into my head: *ha ha ha ha ha ha ha.* I close my eyes and try to push the laugh back out of my brain, but it sticks like a barbed fishhook. I'm tired just thinking of spending time with her and my over-anxious parents.

I know I need to go downstairs, but all I want to do is sit in this room and read. I'm using stacks of magazines to hide the police files and yearbooks. I started my morning combing through them all, looking for clues about Mr. Jerkhin's life. Why send a Makkel to pose as a Science teacher in an Indiana high school? When did he and Eunice figure out the truth about each other? But after a while, the fonts blur and the timelines get fuzzy, and I'm drawn to the bright magazines. I look at these pictures and read about people and places I do not understand. This magazine says "The Stars" are "Just Like Us" and I have no idea how such contradictory statements could be true.

"Deer-dra!" Father shouts. He is standing in the hallway, shouting up toward my room. Mrs. V's laugh chirp chirp chirps up the stairs, digs into my brain.

I slide the police reports under an *US Weekly* with an all-caps headline reading "TOGETHER AGAIN? MAYBE BABY?" and head downstairs.

They're sitting in the kitchen, Mother and Father each with a bottle of wine in front of them and Mrs. V with one in front of her, as well. All bottles are open. It's two in the afternoon.

"There she is!" Mrs. V says. She stands and envelops me in a hug and nearly chokes me with a perfume cloud. For a few moments, everything goes fuzzy and humid and the smell is all I experience. It's like being close to Mr. Jerkhin—that sense of an overwhelming aroma momentarily taking over all other senses, a dull frozen moment in time. I turn down my sensory receptors. Then she pulls back and smiles. She's holding both of my hands and looks at me like I'm something she created and she couldn't be more pleased with her work. "Such a delightful figure!" she says. She taps me on the shoulder: tap tap tap. "I bet the boys are just falling over themselves to get to you!"

Blood rushes to my cheeks, and I shake my head. "Certainly not," I say. It comes out more sad than I intended, and Mrs. V's face twists into a frown.

"Well," she says. "We'll just have to see what we can do about that." I have no idea what this means, and she takes me by the hand and turns to Mother. "Can we use your blow dryer?" she says.

"Oh yes," Mother says. "By all means." She points to the stairs and nods at me. She takes a sip from the wine bottle. Either the wine is getting to her or she and Father have turned their own sensory receptors down far enough to make Mrs. V tolerable. I'm impressed they're still standing. I make a note that we really need to review standard visitation protocols, especially vis-à-vis wine.

"Let's do a little something with that hair," Mrs. V says. "Shall we?"

She chatters away and brushes my hair, and I cannot hear a thing under the high whine of the dryer. She pauses, picks up a curling iron, and then there's a hot push and a pull and she's releasing it, and back to the hair dryer. She repeats this process. In the mirror, my hair is shaping into something resembling the hair of the women in *US Weekly*, and all I can do is stare.

"Honey, you're going to look like a supermodel," Mrs. V says. She curls and releases. "You hide it well, but I just know you have some interesting bone structure under there."

"How are you doing this?" I say. "What are you doing?"

"I'll show you when we're done," she says. "So: high school going okay? You're getting settled in, making a few friends?"

She says it like a question but also not a question. I turn to look at her, and she puts her hands on the sides of my face and steers me back to looking straight at the mirror. "Don't want to burn that pretty face, now," she says.

"School is okay. I am new. It's different than before. I was homeschooled in New Mexico," I say.

"Uh huh," she says. "I've met a few homeschoolers in my day."

"What?" I say.

Her hand grips the crown of my head, turns it straight again. Her fingernails dig lightly into my scalp. "So you're getting along okay, though. Meeting people? Got some projects you're interested in?" She's moved to the other side of my hair. Curl, release, curl, release.

"Sure," I say. "Everyone at school has been very nice. Very accommodating."

"That's just delightful to hear," she says. "We do try to be a good, friendly place for…folks from out of town." She fluffs up the hair near my neck, then pats the top, smooths and brushes, runs a finger up and down my part.

"Everyone has been very kind."

"Good, good." She takes her fingers and separates the curls, turning them from perfect spirals to windblown, messy waves. I should take a photo of this when we're through. This is perfect Popular hair. "Now, you haven't been caught up in any of that unpleasantness with that odd girl that went missing, right? You've been staying away from strangers and those nasty chat rooms on the internet?"

We lock eyes in the mirror, and suddenly I want to grab her hand, to stand up and pull away. But something keeps me in my seat.

"No? No, ma'am. I mean, I know that a girl went missing, but that's all I've heard."

"Wonderful. Marvelous. Well, it's a nasty business. Apparently, some bad foreign actors out at the dairy, if you can believe that." She pauses. "Do you…believe that?"

Her hand tightens slightly on my hair, almost painfully, but not quite. I breathe in deeply. "Dairy cultures, ma'am," I say. "If it's good enough for the FBI…"

She relaxes her grip on my hair, taps at it as if she's petting an animal. "That's a good girl," she says. "No sense digging up old unpleasantness is what I always say. Let sleeping dogs lie. Stay in your lane. And your lane, my dear, is knocking those boys dead out at Danaville High, am I right?" She puts both hands on my head, steers me toward the bedroom mirror. My hair falls in soft curls around my face. It's fairly billowing.

"I don't…" I say.

She runs a hand again down my part, from the top all the way to the bottom. She squeezes my shoulders. "You're welcome, darling," she says. "You just remember our little talk."

Chapter 26
Janitor from Another Planet

We wind our way toward the cafeteria, where students are just beginning to form a line. Well, I wind, he clomps. The smell of cooking food wafts in through my nostrils. I can't always identify particular foods but there's cheese in this dish and this makes the salivary glands in my mouth start up. Macaroni and cheese? Humans are brutally simple beings, but macaroni and cheese makes up for many of their shortcomings. Mother has been experimenting with many variations from her Betty Crocker cookbook, and she has yet to land on one from which I do not derive great pleasure.

I try to ignore the titters from my peers as I follow Jerkhin past the lunch line. He holds a forged note in front of him, as if it offers some explanation why a junior girl would be walking toward the janitor's closet.

I wonder what we would say to a teacher who asked what we're doing. I wonder if his arm will fall off before we get behind closed doors.

He hands me the note as if he's offering some kind of ticket for admission, and then I follow him inside the janitor's closet. The smell hasn't gotten any better. I hold my hand over my face, turn down my sensory receptors. He pulls his arm out of the socket and rests it on the table, the tube of his sleeve twisting unnaturally at the shoulder like the beginnings of a balloon animal. His face is caving in, and when he speaks, it's even hard to understand what he's saying.

"Where is she?" he says. "Eunice."

My mind is reeling, but I try to remember my training. Facts. Science. I am a terranaut first and a high school girl second. "I was going to ask you the same thing," I say. I take my hand away. Even with my sensors dimmed, the smell is nearly unbearable. "Are you…the smell…is your…"

"Biodegrading," he says, the word a mush in his mouth. "Too long. Should have left three years ago."

"But why are you still…" I start, and then I see the look in his eyes, and I realize. "Eunice," I say.

He nods and sits down. The click of silverware on plates chatters in from the lunchroom. I think about the vastness of our mission: two planets, two individuals sent as forward advance across light years of empty blackness, to meet in a stinking closet in Danaville Area High School. Two people with millions depending on them, focusing only on the missing third.

"Were you two…" I start, feeling suddenly ridiculous. "Were you…"

"Friends," he says. He looks out into the lunchroom and quickly reattaches the left arm. "She was. My friend."

I nod and think of Gavin and Barb, how they choose each other for support and company without any ulterior motives. They just like what they are together. How they've let me in, as well. "You picked that up from the humans?" I say.

"It is. Nice," he says. He glances toward the back room, and I know he needs to go recharge whatever is faltering in his biology.

"Look, I don't know what happened to Eunice, but she's why I'm here. Along with the other thing. The Council thing."

"The Council thing," he says. "We need. To talk. About." There's something in his voice, in his crumbling face, that tells me he has ideas that are different from the people who have sent us both here. I wonder what he has in mind. I'm about to ask, when I see the strip of light from the door widen. Someone's coming in.

"Everything okay in here?" Mrs. Queen enters the room, bracelets jangling and crepe shoes creaking. I can't believe we didn't hear her before. "I was just getting some lunch, and it isn't every day I see a student in here with Mr. Jerkhin having such an animated conversation, so…"

Jerkhin grunts and holds his left arm.

"Oh, still trouble with that arm, Mr. Jerkhin?" she says. "I don't know how any of those boys out there can see what football did to your body and still think it's a good idea. But these kids think they'll be young forever. So it goes."

Jerkhin nods and grunts.

Mrs. Queen turns to me. "Everything okay then?"

"Oh yes," I say. "I was just interviewing Mr. Jerkhin for a project."

"Is that so?" she says. Something in her eyes has changed, and it's almost like she's amused, like we are playing some kind of game now. "What class is that, sweetheart?"

"Global Issues. Thanks, Mr. Jerkhin," I say. I almost hold out my hand to shake but notice that he's holding his left arm in place with the right one. I close my notebook and put it back in the backpack. "We will finish that conversation about New Mexico some other time."

Chapter 27
Men in Black

"Deerdra," Father calls up the stairs. "Break-the-fast time."

"Breakfast!" I say. "One word."

"Oatmeal!" Father says.

I look up at the solar system stickers on the ceiling. A joke, but not a joke. Sometimes it's hard to tell, but still, I find them comforting. Eunice Tiffany lay in this same bed. She stared at the same ceiling. I think about Jerkhin and his arm falling out and his body collapsing, biodegrading, his mission completely abandoned, how he may die on this forsaken little planet to find out what happened to her.

Where are you, Eunice?

"Deerdra!" Father shouts.

I roll out of bed and wait a moment as my legs get used to gravity. It's almost normal for me now. Almost.

"I'm coming," I shout and walk to the bathroom. I run the water and that's when I hear the cars outside, the efficient little clamor of expensive car doors closing. The doorbell rings.

I walk downstairs. "What's…" I start.

Somebody knocks on the door, slow and steady. Knock knock knock. Too even and official for Barb or Gavin. Too slow for Mrs. V. Father stands, adjusts his tie, and whispers something to Mother.

Outside, a group loiters on our patio. They are two men and a woman, all of them dressed like Father in dark suits and sunglasses. The men wear hats. The woman wears heels. One of them has horn rims, and I wonder if this is Tim From Work with Glasses. Father's descriptions aren't that creative, but they are accurate. They all stand still, looking straight ahead. An SUV idles in the driveway behind them, painted so dark that it seems to suck light in without reflecting anything back. A woman jogs past the house, trailing a fat Labrador retriever.

Father nods at them and whispers something to Mother. My nervous system has kicked into high gear, and I realize I've been holding my breath. Mother is standing in the corner of the kitchen, a box of Cookie Crisp clutched in her arms like a shield.

"It's okay," Father says as he brushes past. Then he says the code that we've been taught to use only in the most serious of situations, known only to our unit of three.

"I love you."

Father joins the group on the porch. They shake hands but remain silent. I wonder if they are like us, or if they are humans. Father disappears into the SUV, and then it is gone.

I look again to Mother, but she has turned to the dishwasher. "Mother?" I say. "What is happening?" Without thinking, I look at the clock behind her. On top of everything, I'm going to be late for school if I don't leave soon.

"Team leader has initiated the protocol," she says. Her voice is flat, emotionless, as if nothing strange has happened here this morning.

"And that's it? That's all you have for me?" I want to mirror her lack of feeling, but I can't help shouting. For a moment, I wish for a less sophisticated nervous system. It would be better to be Jerkhin, shoving my falling-off arm back into its socket, than to be a teenage girl with this ridiculous gumbo of feelings bubbling around inside me all the time.

"Team leader has initiated the protocol," she repeats. She takes a cookbook out of a drawer and places it on the counter. She places another one on top of it. She takes out the printed recipes that were included in our background dossier. All I can do is stand there and watch. "As second-in-command," Mother says. "I must insist that you also initiate the protocol. I will call the school authorities and tell them that you have a doctor's appointment."

THE I-LOVE-YOU PROTOCOL

This phrase has been chosen due to its frequent usage among Earth Americans and the lack of a correlation in our own, more mature language. "I love you" is used to convey a deep personal regard for another being and translates roughly to "I have a deep personal regard for you."

Usage of the protocol:

This protocol will be officially signaled when Team Lead uses this phrase.

Notes on usage of the protocol:

Keep in mind that it is imperative that team members restrict the usage of this phrase and absolutely do not fall into Earth Americans' habit of using this phrase casually in nearly all interactions.

Notes on the nature of the protocol:

This protocol is preparatory in nature and intended to signal a possible situation that might require retrieval, but it is not in itself the retrieval protocol.

Notes on specific steps of the protocol:

- The protocol is triggered.
- All team members prepare for retrieval: pack federation-issued materials into the assigned "luggage."
- Continue to go about daily mission, maintain interpersonal relationships with contacts and sources, and continue filing reports as necessary.
- If retrieval is required, team members will be contacted via the Retrieval Protocol.
- If retrieval is not required, Team Lead will be signaled from central command, and team activities should return to normal.
- It is essential that all federation-issued materials, such as "clothing" and "personal effects" be returned to their regular positions in order to maintain the appearance of normality among contacts and sources.

Chapter 28
Second-in-Command

We drive to school in silence. Mother is in second-in-command mode, I know—making lists, reviewing protocols. She taps her hands on the wheel and drives faster than usual. Mother said to pack quickly, and not to worry, Father would catch up. I think about my things, all the T-shirts and jeans and skirts and sweaters packed tight into my regulation suitcase, the books and magazines in their cardboard boxes, the electronics full of ridiculous music and television shows and movies. I think about the silver briefcase Mother laid gently on top of my boxes. I've never seen it before.

Per regulations, I will be allowed to retain three items of mission-related personal effects. The rest will be cataloged and destroyed in the ship's atomizer while I'm in suspended animation. If Barb approves, I will take her Clash T-shirt.

Barb. Gavin. Barb and Gavin. If I could take them I would. I can't.

Mother is singing along with the radio, getting the words wrong, tapping her hands on the wheel.

I realize with a jolt what's different about her right now, and my body jumps with adrenaline and anger. "You are happy," I say. I don't really mean for it to come out as an accusation, but there it is.

She slows the car and looks at me, and the second-in-command drops out of her face, and through all of it—the biosuit, and the ridiculous clothing, and the mascara she hasn't gotten the hang of yet, the hairstyle, and the song, and the car, and bright Earth sun beating down on the plush leather, heated seats—it's just Mother again. "You are not?" she says. "Happy? I thought—"

"I don't know. I should be; I mean, I thought I would be happy to finish the mission early, to go home, but I…"

She takes my hand in hers. I can see the school ahead of us now. "I know," she says. "I'm happy you have found comrades."

"Friends."

"Friends," she says. She pulls into the school parking lot and hands me a note. "But one thing you should know," she says. "I think you do know this, deep down, but it is a hard thing to…it is a hard thing."

"What?" I say.

"We can't go home," she says. "Now that we are here, this far, we…Father told you what is happening, I know. Anthea is in its final days. By the time we would get back, there would be no home for us. So, if it is not here, then it is the next place."

"What would the next place be?"

"A ship? A number of ships? Another planet? We are not the only mission. I hope it will be here."

I don't know what I hope. I like it here, but I like it here and now. Gavin and Barb, and their friend who was homeschooled in New Mexico, who's definitely not an alien from a planet considering taking over the Earth. If the rest of Anthea came to Earth, it would be so different. Like two bubbles touching together. Would they merge into one, or would they both burst?

"But never home," Mother says. And then she says it again, and I have the feeling that she's just getting used to the idea herself. "Never home."

* * *

I drift into school and drop my note on Mrs. Queen's desk. I don't even hear what she says as I turn around and head toward the hallway. There's another tinkle that I know is her voice, and then she says my name, low, and I turn around.

"You okay, honey?" she says. She puts a hot and sticky hand on my arm. "Visitor issues?" She smiles as if we're sharing an inside joke.

"Visitor?" I say. Does she know? Is it that obvious? Have we been found out already? How do I enact an I Love You protocol from school when Father is nowhere to be found?

She leans in closer. "Your period, honey," she says.

"Oh," I say. Blood rushes to my cheeks—I can't tell if they're the ones in my biosuit or my own face—as I remember. A particularly cruel and basic part of their supposedly evolved anatomy. "Yes," I say.

"Okay," she says, her voice hushed. "We don't need to broadcast it to the entire school. You let me know if you need anything."

For some reason, she hugs me, and I walk down the hallways with the scent of her perfume—was it the same as one worn by Mrs. V or am I just conflating two recent issues of heavily perfumed women randomly hugging me?—ringing in my olfactory senses. I want to turn my sensors down, but I need to be on alert today.

This could be my last day in school. I will see Barb at lunch, Gavin at Calc. I know I'm forbidden to say anything, and this is somewhat of a comfort. What would I say? Where could I possibly start?

Everything seems brighter, bigger, more colorful. The last time I felt this way, we were on the ship, just slipping into the wormhole, Mother lying exhausted on the floor, Father kneading her forehead.

I know that this is a trick of my nervous system. Maybe a feedback loop in my biosuit. I know that my superior intelligence, thousands of years of evolution past this silly species with their ridiculous clothing and customs, their waiting lines and pop songs and trivial, tribal customs, should dull the effects of these emotions. I've been trained and understand that most of the emotions I'm feeling are actually indicators of the less advanced status of this species, the fact that they are evolved enough to understand evolution but not enough to comprehend how rudimentary a species they truly are. But right now, it's like a wall that stands between me and clarity. I see the wall. I understand the wall. But I still cannot get past the wall any more than I can think it away.

Damn sympathetic nervous system. Damn advanced military engineering. I wonder if Mr. Jerkhin has this problem. But he has other problems, with his degrading arm and his stink and his time running out. Jerkhin. I realize that he's the only one who might possibly understand what is happening right now, and also the best option we had for finding Eunice Tiffany.

I sneak into the cafeteria and look for his door. It's half-closed and I can see his silhouette filling the space. He teeters to the side, holds the door for balance, teeters to the other side. He steps through and looks at the wall, pauses briefly when he sees me. He falls to the ground.

Chapter 29
Almost Like Normal

I knock on Gavin's door. I've only been here with Barb, and then only briefly—rolling up in Barb's old Chevrolet, which is possibly more rust spray and bumper sticker than actual car at this point—and it feels almost like a betrayal. If you didn't know what was going on, you might just think this was a girl knocking on a boy's door, maybe coming over for dinner or to go out on a regular, old Friday-night date. A stray beam from the setting sun catches in the side mirror of the truck I've parked in the driveway and flares a fiery orange. From inside, I hear rustling and then the low hum of a vacuum cleaner. I hear Gavin shouting, his annoyance clear even through the door and the cleaner's dull roar.

Finally, the vacuum shuts down, and a person comes to the door. "Hello, Deerdra!" Gavin's mother says. She seems thinner than before, the skin pulled tight around her tan face. Her blonde hair cascades down her shoulders like the women in the Real Housewives shows. I try to remember which location. Gavin's mother looks most like the women from Orange County. Or like Mrs. V. Behind her, the house is spotless. Music plays from somewhere. "Gavin!" she calls up the stairs. "You have a visitor!"

"How did you know it was me?" I say.

"Oh silly," she says and waves a hand as if the answer to my question is obvious. She holds up a plate full of cookies, arranged artfully on a bright ceramic tray. "Cookie?"

"No, thank you," I say.

She takes a step back and regards me, looking up and down. "Such an adorable figure!" she says. "I was kind of hoping…" And then she shakes her head quickly and holds the cookie tray out, and I have a feeling that it isn't optional anymore. I take one. Upstairs, I can hear scuffle, Gavin muttering at some article of clothing that isn't cooperating.

If my people really are taking over, they should lead with the sarisuits. They just make so much more sense.

"So, are you kids going somewhere exciting?"

"Oh, I don't know," I say. "Probably just, you know, go to the mall or something." Finally, I'm able to put some of my research to good use. "We were going to, you know, just hang out, walk around, see the kids from the other high schools, maybe go to the record…" But something stops me—a look in her eye, quizzical and intense.

"That's terrific," she says, but her voice is flat. I fear I have said something wrong.

"Mom, it's so gross to make comments about my friend's figure."

Thank goodness. Gavin.

Gavin trots down the stairs, and I turn to say goodbye to his mother. She's standing to the side, leaning against the wall, one hand held up as if to prevent herself from dropping in a heap to the carpet. She shakes her head. "I just can't…" she says.

I'm frozen. I feel like I should do something, but what would I do? There are scenarios where I could hug her, sing a song, give her a long, romantic kiss, sneak out the door, make a wisecrack. A door closes in another room, and ice tinkles into a glass. Something pours. At this, Gavin's mother bounces back into position, her back lengthening into a perfect posture, her hair flouncing back into golden ripples. She runs her hands down the sides of the dress, and it flattens around her. Her figure is also adorable, but this isn't a comment a younger person should say to an older person. *Don't stand out.*

"Oh, hello there." A man is standing in the doorway now—grey hair, distinguished. He looks like a lawyer on a syndicated TV show. Not the main one but the one who helps the main one, the one who is a little older and has seen some things and perhaps made some mistakes that will be a shocking reveal in a two-part special.

"Oh, Deerdra and Gav were just going to run over to the mall and… What did you say it was you were going to do, dear?" Gavin's mother speaks a little too fast, too bright. In this moment, she reminds me of Mother.

"Hi. John Neary," he says. He reaches his hand out to shake. His hand is cool and strong.

"Deerdra Grey," I say. "I am new. I am pleased to…I was just picking up Gavin to go…hang out at the mall."

"Well, that's nicé," he says. "Hey, would you kids like to stay…"

"Mom! Dad!" Gavin shouts from the doorway. "Let her go."

"Some other time," Gavin's father says. "It was very nice to meet you."

"Sorry," he says. "I don't get many visitors and they just…you know."

"Oh yes," I say. "I totally know how that can be. Parents just don't understand."

Gavin's father laughs. "Right," he says. "So, you're headed downtown to the Gallery Mall?"

"No," I say as Gavin and I head outside. "The Tulip Tree Mall. I didn't know there was a Gallery Mall in the area?"

Gavin's father laughs as he waves us off and closes the door. I laugh, too, even though I don't know what he's laughing at. Humans place so much importance on humor.

Jerkhin's truck looms in the driveway. Hints of his decomposing biosuit and the pine-tree air freshener hanging from the rearview mirror waft out through the open windows. I need more range than our bikes can provide and calling a car would broadcast our location. To Mother and Father, to Mrs V, to a black helicopter, to Anthea…I don't know how far it could go. I just know I need my friend.

I hope I've made Gavin laugh enough in the last few months. I need him to trust me.

We climb in, and Gavin looks at me with questions in his eyes. He smiles. "Nice ride. I didn't think you had your license."

"I need you to help me with something."

"At the mall?"

"Not quite. Gavin…can I trust you? Like with something big?"

The questions in his eyes double, then disappear as he looks at me, sees I'm serious. "Yeah. Of course. To the moon and back."

Interesting choice of words.

I start the engine.

Chapter 30
There's Something I Should Tell You

The drive to school reminds me of traveling through the wormhole. Time shifts and words blur, and I perform the essential duties to keep the vehicle on course while time and light and my thoughts swirl around me. In this case, essential duties are nodding and smiling and frowning appropriately as Gavin tells me about a song that's on the radio. How his parents used to dance to it in the kitchen. Then things got rough, but Gavin still likes the song.

Soon we're at school, parking in the football booster lot. The flowers are lovely. I walk toward the school, and Gavin follows. I try not to think about why I went straight to Gavin, didn't even think about getting Barb, as well, but it's as simple as this: I knew he would follow. I knew he wouldn't ask questions until I was ready to give answers. A dark part of me knew I could use him. Mother would be proud. Father would be…I don't know. Colonel Muckinzee may give me a commendation and a mixtape.

We slip inside. My heart is pounding, and I assume Gavin's is, as well. I hope Jerkhin is still humanoid. I don't know what I'll tell Gavin if Jerkhin's biosuit is destroyed if he's in his Makkelian form.

The fluorescent lights buzz overhead. Tentacles of stench grope into my nostrils, writhe into my brain. He can't be well.

But Jerkhin is gone. There's no way to hide that form, all three hundred or so wheezing, smelling pounds of him, but I look under the table, behind the desk, out in the hallway. At the very least, I expect to find the arm.

"Ugh. He was definitely here. He should see a doctor." Gavin says. He's pulled his T-shirt over his mouth and nose as a makeshift mask. He wanders out into the cafeteria. "God, I hate this place."

I take a few steps toward him, and suddenly I'm in the air, and for a moment it's lovely, like floating in the regeneration chamber, and then there's pain everywhere, and I'm on the ground. Gavin is above me. He reaches an arm out and hesitates, just for a split second, before he grabs my hand. I'm flooded with another feeling. Love? Friendship? "I'm okay," I say. "Just…give me a minute."

His eyes run down my body, checking for injuries. My face is hot, my fingers tingle, and my toes feel numb. Did I crush a thermoregulator on my biosuit? He helps me stand, and for a moment, it's hard to breathe. I let go of his hand and make a mental note to run a diagnostic as soon as I'm home.

"I don't want to think about what that is," Gavin says. He waves his free hand at the ground where I slipped.

The trail leads from the floor to the back room, to Jerkhin's regeneration chamber. The wave of heat dissipates—something may be malfunctioning, but it's not broken. "Oh, thank goodness," I say.

"Not the reaction I thought you were going to have," Gavin says.

"No," I say. "I think he's in there."

"In that room?"

I nod.

"In the janitor sex room?"

"What!?" Makkels reproduce asexually. Would they have added that function in his biosuit?

"What Barb and I assume. Dark, smells weird, he's always in a better mood when he comes out. I know you missed some things in homeschool, but I may have to show you the parts of the internet beyond your parental restrictions."

I stand up and walk to the door. It's cool to the touch, and I imagine the feeling, the floating, the pink edges peeking beneath the grey, just like home. I knock. Knock knock knock.

"You are not going to go in that sex room." Gavin's voice floats over my shoulder. "It's the Janitor Sex Room, Deerdra. The name kind of says it all."

"Wait," I say. I picture him floating down, all of that mass no longer weighed down by gravity. I wait, hoping for him to invite us in.

"This is going to be fine. 'Gavin, how was the mall?' 'Well actually, Dad, we skipped the mall and went to the Janitor Sex Room instead,'" Gavin says. He's trying to be funny but there's an edge in his voice.

The knob turns. Gavin takes a step back and I realize in a flash how poorly prepared he is for this moment. How poorly prepared I am, for that matter. The door swings open, and Jerkhin is standing there, holding his arm in his right hand. "It's done," he says.

He lumbers out of the room and closes the door, using the good hand that still clasps the bad arm to drive the latch closed. Goes pale, starts sweating.

"What is…" Gavin says. He backs up to the wall.

I stand between them, Jerkhin collapsed against the wall, his arm sliding out of his hand and onto the floor. It twitches like a dying thing. There's no protocol for this. I'm not going to receive a commendation or a mixtape.

"Gavin," I say. "There's something I should tell you."

Chapter 31
Homeschooled in New Mexico

"So…we're your science experiment?" Gavin says. We're sitting on the steps outside the school, staring at the cars as they pass. Trying to be ordinary students having an ordinary conversation. Ignoring the beat-up truck parked in the booster parking lot.

It's getting dark and the sky is pink and grey, but the ratios are all wrong as usual. This ridiculous place with its functional sun and only marginally ruined sky.

"No." He's so much more than that. But I think of the pre-mission briefings, the reports I've beamed back to the Colonel. Of whatever Mother and Father do with their days. "Well, sort of. I'm really sorry," I say. I'm experiencing what Colonel Muckinzee refers to as a cocktail of emotions. I don't understand why Mother's housewives would drink actual cocktails to feel this way. But all the yelling finally makes sense.

"No, it's okay," he says, and I can tell that he means it. That he's surprised that he means it. He pauses, listens to the moans emanating from the cab of the truck. And the snoring.

"In a weird way, I kind of get it? I mean, I've always felt like I missed the day that they handed out the scripts. We're in another reboot of another shitty eighties high school movie, and the jocks and the cheerleaders and the popular kids and the losers are all playing their roles. Like everyone around me knows who they are and what they want and who they want, and I'd just…observe."

Humans use humor to handle uncertain situations. Strange, since the best jokes are unpredictable. I have read about theories of humor, but I know I'm not advanced enough to pull it off. But there was one chapter in Father's manual that may help—the Dad Joke. "So now that you believe in aliens, you can try believing in yourself? Huh, Sport?" I say, grazing a punch off his arm. It works at least a little because he laughs and pushes at my hand in a way that I believe could be called "fond."

"This actually explains some things, to be honest. You, too. I mean, your cover wasn't exactly airtight. Homeschooled in New Mexico?"

"New Mexico is a very different place."

"New Mexico—*your* New Mexico—is how far away?"

"My New Mexico is very far away. Six thousand light years, give or take."

"And Eunice Tiffany."

"Also homeschooled in New Mexico, yes."

"And the janitor. And the janitor's left arm."

"Homeschooled. Especially his left arm, homeschooled from a very early age."

"But not in…*New Mexico* New Mexico, though, right?"

"Yes." I remember Father's admonition; they're not an equal species. "More like…homeschooled in Arizona. But like, an octopus homeschooled in Arizona. Smart octopus! But not at the level of my…homeschool."

A woman walks by with a small dog. She's talking to it in a funny voice: "Good girl, Libby, good girl, let's keep on walking now, Libby…" We pause and watch, and for a second, it's almost like everything is normal, almost like I haven't breached the most important part of our protocol, like Father isn't missing and Mother isn't at home packing up our entire mission for possible retreat. I wonder what that would mean. Our dying planet.

"So, what now?" Gavin says. "What about Barb?"

"Barb, I…" I have no idea how to answer this question. "Give me a few days? This part isn't in the manual."

"And the part where we need to find your fellow homeschooled New Mexican?"

"That's why I was at the school, with Jerkhin, to begin with. He was friends with Eunice. Either he knows where she is or he's afraid…afraid his viable time in this atmosphere may also be coming to an end."

"Now that," Gavin says, "sounds like an alien. Or New Mexicans talk like awkward scientists."

I laugh, and I'm flooded with relief. There's a chance my breach of protocol will not be disastrous. A chance I will get away with this. A chance that I will find Eunice Tiffany. But I'm going to have to go off-mission and trust some humans with my secret. This is certainly not the conclusion that would be drawn by Father or Mother or Colonel Muckinzee, but it may have been another agent's choice.

"So…Eunice," I say.

"Yeah?"

"You said Kayla was her best friend, right? They had gotten pretty close in the past year?"

"Definitely. It was weird, to be honest."

"Weird how?"

"They just didn't fit the script, you know? Like I was saying before, everybody here is playing their role, doing what they would be doing if they were in some stupid teen movie. But those two hanging together, eating lunch, talking, whatever. It just didn't fit. They were in some other movie."

"Hmm."

"I don't know if I like the sound of that hmm," he says.

"I think it's time to get our Harry Potter on."

"Get our Harry Potter on?" Gavin's brow furrows as he tries to source the reference. We had been told that those stories were as close to a universal experience as you could find on Earth, the modern-day equivalent of Zeus and Olympus. But maybe things have changed.

"Yes. Books one through three. Maybe book four."

"We're going to binge everything in one sleepless weekend, like third graders? My wand's been collecting dust for a while, Deerdra."

"We're going to focus on the solvable mystery in front of us and hope it leads to the bigger plot eventually."

"Kayla?"

"Kayla."

"What about your, what did you say, homeschooled octopus from Arizona?"

"I need to catch up with him later, too. But he needs to stay in that regeneration chamber for a few more hours."

Gavin's fingers clutch at the cool concrete stairs, and he stares off at the truck, then beyond. I worry that it's suddenly too much. Aliens regenerating their disintegrating limbs. A new friend from a few states away is from a few galaxies away.

We come in peace. I'm not saying it was aliens, but it was aliens. Resistance is futile. You will be assimilated. I want to believe. All fun slogans for a t-shirt, loved until the novelty wears off and then tossed in the closet next to a magic wand that lost its magic. But now I'm begging him to believe. And to believe that not all of us come in peace.

"One condition," he says.

"Anything."

"I'm Hermione."

The setting sun is suddenly a comfortable grey with pink edges. It feels like home.

"Gavin, my friend," I say. "For the rest of this, whatever it is, we can all be Hermione."

Chapter 32
Walk it Back

William parks the car and stares at the house glowing in front of him. The blinds are drawn, but still, he can see the light within. *There is a metaphor in there somewhere,* he thinks. There was a time when he would have written something down, returned to it later to try to make a poem. That time is over, at least for now. And then he thinks that they've followed protocol, and following protocol is always good, always best. Someday, he will return to his poetry, his little notebooks, but for now, his most important role, as he has been reminded during the three-day retreat, is Mission Leader.

"I'm home!" he says, coming through the door. He flashes on the training materials. This is how a father comes home to his family. He is following protocol and following protocol is always best.

Deerdra runs down the stairs and hugs him. She is crying. "Where were you? What happened? Who were those people? Are you okay?" She pulls back and then punches him in the arm. "You scared me!"

She has taken to this assignment better than either of us, he thinks, *actually acting like an Earth teenager.*

"You are back," Stefanie says. She stands in the doorway to the kitchen, wiping her hands on a dish towel. "We will walk back the I Love You Protocol?"

"Correct," William says. "It was a more or less standard meeting. A retreat. Some of the regulars and also Tim From Work with Glasses. I was unsure if they were taking me to… I was unsure if it was regular work or if they had found out. Protocol dictates that…"

"I know what protocol dictates," Stefanie says. She turns and walks back to the kitchen. So, she really wanted to abandon the mission. William notes this the way he noted the metaphor—something to be saved, remembered, something that may be important later. He will need to work on the morale of his team. He has been trained for this, of course, warned that initiation and then abandonment of a protocol may often result in confusion, questioning, declining team morale. Perhaps they will go to the all-you-can-eat Indian buffet for lunch tomorrow, or to the movies, or to the arcade to play the silly machine games the Earth people like so much.

Deerdra squeezes his arm, the same one she had punched a moment ago. "I'm happy you are home," she says.

William squeezes her back. "So am I," he says.

Chapter 33
Is This What We're Doing Here?

"You're so good at all of this," I say, swirling my grande skim cappuccino in movements that mirror Kayla's own constant swirling on the other side of the little table. Swirl swirl swirl.

"All of..." Kayla says.

"Everything," I say. "The hair and outfits and school and...everything."

"I know," she says, testing the temperature of her drink with a sip. "I mean, I know it looks like that."

Flattery can be used with humans to gain almost anything. Even the most self-aware can often be rendered vulnerable with this tactic. It's one of the most obvious things about them—embarrassingly easy. I almost hold off on pressing this button further but with everything happening, I don't know how much longer I have to work on this mission. "Oh, it most definitely does," I say. She laughs and I laugh with her. I have no idea what's funny. "To be honest, I was hoping you could help me out a little."

"Help you out?"

"I know. It's maybe a surprising thing to ask. Or maybe not, if you take a look at my hair and my clothes, my...conversational style? I don't know how to do certain things that you know. My mother—I don't know how you know these things, but I cannot rely on her to help. She's not from this place. She's learning, herself, how to do much of it from the *Cosmopolitan* magazines."

"Your mother still reads magazines?"

"I'm afraid so."

"Me too! Every week we get *Us Weekly, Entertainment Weekly,* some other something weekly that I can't even keep track of. It's like the Kardashian Family News Service. I can't even."

We have established a rapport. This is an important step. I didn't even know if she would acquiesce to my request to get coffee together. I don't really know why she did. But here we are.

"So maybe you could help me…fit in okay? A little better?"

"Well…you fit in pretty well already. I mean, we're here, right?"

I nod and sip at my drink. It's warm and sour and sweet and delicious. I can feel the caffeine's desirable effect on my nervous system, a slight uptick in my bodily registers, the light feeling of energy in my head. I understand why Colonel Muckinzee has suggested that we stay away from this particular drug, as it may become habit-forming. "Thank you," I say. "But still, I wonder how…for instance, you chose that shirt that you're wearing. It is very…cute?"

She takes a sip of her own drink and cocks her head. "Deerdra, is this what we're doing here? Is this really what we're doing here? Talking about my top? That's not really what we're doing here, is it? I mean, I know it seems like I have the whole high-school-popular-girl thing happening, and I do have 11,245 Instagram followers and I'm only seventeen, but I also have a 4.0 and I've read everything Margaret Atwood has ever written. I just read *Wise Blood* for the second time this summer. I have enough AP credits already to be a second-semester college freshman."

I open my bag to find a notebook to write down "Margaret Atwood" and "Wise Blood," but then I catch myself. I try flattery again. "You are very pretty and smart," I say.

She takes another sip of her drink, and I find that I'm unconsciously imitating her. A very interesting development. "Let's go with smart and then pretty," she says.

"Smart and pretty," I say. "In that order."

"So," she says. "Now that we established that, let me say I'm smart enough to have a sense for how smart you are. Smart enough to know you have some regular little CSI stuff going on with the janitor and your buddies. Smart enough to know you invited me here to talk about Eunice."

"Eunice Tiffany," I say. "Yes." I reach for my bag, and this time, I do open it. I take out the folder. I slide it across the table.

Chapter 34
Le Big Mac

Barb slides in next to me. She bumps me with her hip, bump bump, and opens the container labeled Big Mac. "Mmmmm," she says. "It's like a hamburger but also not really a hamburger, but it's also kind of better than a normal hamburger? You know?" She pops a French fry in her mouth and regards the cheeseburger. "It's like a cheeseburger aliens would make if they, like, learned about Earth from watching TV shows and movies, like a cheeseburger from Galaxy Quest."

Gavin chokes on his soda, Diet Coke exploding out of his nose. Barb swipes the Big Mac off the table and regards it carefully. Gavin is still snorting, blowing his nose with a napkin. I'm frozen.

"Damn, Gav," Barb says. "Kindly keep your coke snot out of my perfect alien burger."

He snorts again and looks at me.

"I need to try one of these," I say. "Alien burgers."

Gavin shakes his head.

"They didn't have McDonalds in New Mexico?" Barb says. "Sometimes I think you came here from, like, New Mexico in 1950."

"Homeschooled in New Mexico," Gavin says. "Might as well be from Mars or something."

When I tell her, she's going to think this is hilarious. Or annoying. Probably annoying. I feel a swell of pride. I've been able to possibly accurately predict how a human teenager will react to a complicated and emotional interpersonal situation. I have intuitively managed the complicated algorithm, or more accurately the web of human reaction.

"So," Barb says. "What's happening with our little caper?"

Gavin looks at me. I look at Barb.

"You two have been colluding," she says. "So what's happening, Woodward and Bernstein?"

"I met with Kayla," I say.

"You looking to increase your social status, get some more Instagram followers?" Barb says. "Hey, did she take any selfies? Were you in them? Did she take a picture of her coffee and then post it and then throw it away and go do Pilates or something?"

"No, but this is an enjoyable line of questioning," I say. Now, I'm not so sure what she'll do when I tell her the truth about me. She is an enigma, impossible to predict, even for a talented and trained agent from an advanced society. But, I hear Father's voice in my head: *She is still an Earth being.* "She was…okay actually?"

"*Kayla Rogers: Okay Actually.* I think that might be her next campaign slogan for homecoming queen."

"Like she needs a slogan," Gavin says. He steals one of Barb's fries.

"Who needs a slogan when you have thirteen-thousand-something Instagram followers, am I right?" Barb says. Gavin reaches for another fry, and she slaps his hand. She takes a bite of the Big Mac. "Oh, jeepers cats, that is a good sandwich. Nice work, aliens." She points to the ceiling and gives the thumbs-up.

"She did say Eunice had been nervous about something, something she couldn't talk about, or wouldn't, with Kayla."

"Something, or somebody?"

"Maybe both?"

"Like a bigfoot janitor who smells like rocket fuel and sweat and orange juice, maybe?"

I consider how much to tell her. Gavin won't return my gaze. Just a few moments ago, I was so proud of myself and my ability to make these many computations in my head, to predict human behavior. I have a long way to go. "There's something…" I start, but then both Gavin and Barb are staring behind me. They are both silent, watching somebody approach. The mood at the table, carefree and casual, has changed immediately, like we've been caught in a quick emotional rainstorm.

"Hey," Kayla says. "Scooby Gang scoobying it up, huh?"

"Hey, Kayla," I say.

She sits down, and Barb and Gavin shift in their seats. It's really quite interesting how the group physically reorganizes itself in the presence of an alpha. Barb puts her Big Mac down and scoots up closer. "Hello, my name is Barbara," she says. "I am a student in the high school that you attend."

Kayla takes one of her French fries and pops it in her mouth. "Cute," she says. "I guess you don't remember third grade, the thing at recess? My green shirt and green pants and…" She drifts off, and something changes, seems to harden. "Never mind," she says. "It is what it is."

"Oh, you should Instagram that," Barb says. She moves her food out of reach for Kayla.

"Insta-bite me," Kayla says, but she's smiling.

"I mean, so deep. It is what it is," Barb says. "Did you make that up? You seem so, what it is the word…so woke."

Kayla turns to Gavin. "Hey, Gav," she says. "Hope you're doing okay." Her voice has softened. Gavin is turning slightly pink, and I wonder if the reaction is sexual or embarrassment or something in between. "Haven't seen you at church in a while, but I know the whole…you know. I get it. Hope your mom is okay?"

"Thanks," Gavin says. "More my dad you need to worry about, if you know what I mean."

Kayla opens her bag and fishes for something. "Well," she says. "This repartee has been really great, but I have something…I don't know. It's probably nothing." She puts a postcard on the table but keeps her hand over it. She turns to me. "I can trust you? I mean, all of you?" she says.

"You're not going to try to get us to join the Church of Scientology, are you?" Barb says.

Kayla takes the postcard and puts it back in her bag. "This was a mistake. This was… Jesus, you're still such a bully."

"Me a bully?" Barb says.

Kayla stops and just stares at her. Gavin picks at his cuticles. He looks like he's going to cry. I'm experiencing a strange emotion that I cannot identify and then realize it's disappointment.

Earth beings sometimes respond to challenges. They don't like to admit that they cannot do something. They don't like to admit that their own personal failings, quirks, emotions might lead them to behave in a way that's nonproductive in terms of goal achievement.

"It's okay," I say. "We were never going to find out what happened to her anyway. I mean, look at us." I stand. "Maybe I will try one of these Big Macs, and then we can all go walk around the mall and eat gummy bears."

"Deerdra…" Gavin says. The question is clear in his voice, in his eyes. He wipes at a tear and blows his nose in a McDonald's napkin.

"You two don't even care enough about Eunice Tiffany to get past, what was it you said, the recess incident? Third grade? To get past the fact that Kayla here sits at one table at lunch and we sit at another? I am new here. I know that. I know it's a lot to get past, so if you can't get past it, let's go, let's give up on all this Harry

Potter nonsense and go do some normal teenager things, have some visceral experiences like walking around the mall." I stand and pretend to be gathering my things.

"Is this the part where I say wait, you're wrong, we can do it, we will do it by gum. Or something like that?" Barb says.

I wait a beat, look at Gavin, at Kayla, and finally back to Barb. "Yes, this is that part."

"Wait you're wrong we can do it we will do it," she says in a flat monotone. "By gum."

"I'm actually down with that," Kayla says. "If you are."

Barb nods. "Sorry about third grade," she says.

"Maybe not so down with the part where we say 'by gum' now that I think about it," Kayla says.

"I kick it old school," Barb says. She nods at Kayla. "So what you got there in the way of a clue?"

Kayla reaches back into the bag and places a postcard on the table. It's from a place called City Lights Books. She flips it over. Kayla's address is printed out and taped in the address portion. In the other, nothing but a typed-out smiley face: :-).

"San Francisco?" Gavin says.

"Why do you think it's from her?" Barb says.

I stare at that smiley face, remember what I saw in the corner of the home room next to Jerkhin's name and the Makkel universe: :-).

"I guess…" Kayla says. "Well, I don't know it's from her. I mean, I do get postcards every now and then from, like, my grandmother, but she always writes my name longhand and puts a note: Loving Taos. Wish you were here. Grandma stuff, you know?"

Barb and Gavin shake their heads, and I follow. Grandma stuff? I will have to consult my documentation if this is going to be a part of the project.

"So this just comes to my house with no anything, just this smiley face, and it's from City Lights in San Francisco, and the first person I thought of was Euney. I mean, she was kind of…she didn't want many people to know because it's not, like, cool or whatever. Well, it's just definitely not cool. But she was kind of a…hippie? As much as, like, a sixteen-year-old girl could possibly be one?"

"A hippie?" Gavin says.

"I know, right?" Kayla says. "But yeah, she kind of was? Like she was super into Conservation Science and some of those old hippie bands and the whole deal. So when this thing comes, she's been gone, she used to do the smiley face—I mean everybody does the smiley face, but it was kind of her thing."

I flash on that handwriting in the corner: Jerkhin :-).

"So…what do we do with this?" Gavin says. He looks at me. Then Barb looks at me. Then Kayla. Somehow, I have become the leader of this group. Very interesting. I believe Colonel Muckinzee would approve.

"I think we need to talk to the janitor," I say.

"Back to the janitor?" Barb says.

"They were friends. Or something," Kayla says.

"Back to the janitor," I say.

Chapter 35
Ice Cream Date

We pull up to the Dairy Queen, and Gavin stops the car. "Oh God, I feel like I'm dropping my little girl off on her first date," he says.

"Well…" I say.

"Oh God no, Deerdra," he says, and we both laugh.

"Seriously?" I say, the giggles escaping like the tiny bubbles in the drink they call soda. "Seriously, this is almost certainly my first and last date."

Gavin chokes on a laugh, and I follow, and then we are both in tears, red, heat filling up the already warm center of the BMW. It isn't even very funny but the feeling of it, of the tension escaping my body, my tear ducts activating and my larynx contracting, the oxygen rushing in and out of my bio layer, the sound of my friend giggling and spurting, it builds on itself until finally we are both spent and breathing heavily.

"Well," I say. "That was as advertised. We're not really supposed to do much of that. Or we are briefed that the experience will be exhilarating and exhausting. Confusing."

"You are briefed?"

"Oh, we are briefed."

"But you haven't…laughed? Since you've been here?"

He seems sad, and I wonder again at what a complicated and strange species they are. "I have. Sometimes. Just not like that. What we are here for, how we spend most of our time, it is…well, it isn't very funny." I wonder what Mother and Father would do if they saw this scene play out, whether they would commend my work fitting in or send an immediate reprimand down through the chain of command. I wonder that I don't seem to care.

"Anyway," he says, pointing toward the little store and the picnic tables beyond. "There squats your young New Mexican homeschooled suitor."

I see Jerkhin sitting by himself at the table farthest from the road. He is licking at a comically large ice cream cone, vanilla, long and pointy and dripping. It's a miracle of Earth engineering that the table he's sitting at hasn't tipped over. He stares up at a point where the trees meet the woods, and I wonder if he's spotted an interesting bird, or if he's been frozen by a glitch in his biosuit, and then I see the moon peeking grey and glowing over the tree line, and I understand.

"Okay," I say, surprised at the huskiness in my voice, the real affection and concern I feel for the strange janitor from Makkel, of all places. "I should go."

"You're sure you don't want me to stay?" Gavin says. "I mean you may need some muscle." He makes a face like he's serious, and I laugh and feel the affection flood through the sympathetic nervous system.

"I'll be okay," I say. "Besides, you know, this is, how would you say it? Alien business."

"Alien business?" Gavin says. "Just another day in Danaville."

The car pulls away, and Jerkhin turns. He looks terrible, grey and sweaty, and falling apart. I wonder if the left arm is even attached or just hanging loose inside his flannel shirt. I sit down.

"Not even going. To get. Ice cream?" he says, taking a lick from his cone.

"Not really hungry," I say. "And also, the cold foods? Do you know why they would do that? It just doesn't…it grosses me out. Cold food?"

He takes another lick and stares back at the place where the trees meet the sky. The moon is just emerging, starting to glow more white than grey, morphing from what we might see on our dying planets to this relatively healthy one, a miracle of clear sky that could only belong to an adolescent planet. "Going to. Miss. This," he says.

"It is pretty," I say. "A little bright for my taste, a little, what do they say, new money?"

"The ice cream. I'm going. To miss. Ice cream. Soft serve. Vanilla."

"You don't have anything like that at home?" I say.

He turns and looks at me. His face twists into a smile. I wonder if his left eyeball is going to pop out, and somehow it stays rooted in place. "We both know. I'm not. Going home."

"I just…"

"Come on," he says. He wheezes, a great exhale like a donkey's bray, wheezes in and out and in and out, and finally starts coughing. He holds his left arm, and I'm more sure than ever that it's just hanging there, attached to the shirt and not the shoulder. People at the other tables stare and whisper. Finally, the fit subsides, and he breathes heavily, his shirt soaked through with sweat. The chemical smell is becoming overwhelming, and my sympathetic nervous system is sending flight instincts to my brain. "She wasn't. Like that," he says.

I sit up. "She? Eunice Tiffany?"

"Of course," he says.

"So look," I say. "If you don't have long, then it's more important than ever that I know...what you know."

"We were. Friends," he says. "We both...I don't know. Liked it. Here?" He looks at me, and I can see the sadness and desperation on his face despite the poor engineering.

"So you won't be going home?" I say. His face says everything. "I'm sorry," I say.

"I made. A decision." He takes another lick at his ice cream cone. His hands are covered in drips.

"Did she make the same one?" I ask.

He stands, balances himself on the table, and drops the cone into a nearby garbage can. "I don't know," he says.

"Are you sure she didn't just get called back?"

"She was. Scared. Of going. Home. And scared. Of not."

"And you..."

Two cars pull into the Dairy Queen parking lot in unison, moving quickly, their tires scraping on the gravel. Jerkhin stands quickly, and before I know what's happening, he's walking toward the woods, standing under the white moon and motioning for me to follow.

I hear talking, a familiar voice. "Run," Jerkhin says quickly and quietly. He jogs into the forest, moving faster than I've seen him move, dragging the left leg but still running. I turn and see people coming my way, register a number of figures in business clothing progressing quickly, smiling, acting as if they're striding toward a handshake. I follow Jerkhin into the woods. "Run," he says. "This is not. Not good. We need to get away."

I've almost caught up to him. The woods are dark and cold. I can hear the breath in my chest, my footfalls crackling through the brush. Jerkhin's arm falls off, and I pause to pick it up. In the distance, footsteps getting closer.

"Leave it!" Jerkhin says. I step over the arm and follow him farther into the woods.

Chapter 36
Pew! Pew Pew Pew!

I follow Jerkhin deeper into the forest. It's getting dark, dark enough for me to feel almost comfortable running through branches and trees. He veers right, and I follow, hopping over a downed tree, landing in mud, and still running. I wish I could release some of the gravity in my suit and really fly, but we learned early on that the technology has grown only as far as needed to maintain the appearance of our Earth selves. I can hear Jerkhin wheezing, could probably follow him by smell if need be. Behind us, people are moving, quieter than us, businesslike. They have flashlights of some kind—a pale green light that bounces in and out of my peripheral vision. Jerkhin pulls himself into a stand of trees and starts fishing through his pockets, of course with his right arm as his left one is still likely twitching and shaking at the edge of the woods.

"Reach," he says, and then wheezes. "Into." Wheeze. He points to his back left pocket. "In there."

I think about what Gavin said before he dropped me at the car: *Your first date.*

"Okay," I say. "But this better not turn out to be…" I fumble in his pocket, pick through lint and some papers and something sticky that I hope is a candy wrapper. He's still wearing his janitor's uniform, and the pockets are very deep. I realize this may not be a standard Earth uniform. "What am I looking for?"

"Little bigger…than a pen," he says. He leans against a tree. All of his extremities have begun shaking.

Finally, I find it, just as he described—a long, smooth object. It's slightly larger than a pen and smaller than a banana. It feels useful, heavy, well-made. I stare at it. I have nothing like this, and although I don't know what it does yet, I find myself jealous, angry that I have not been similarly equipped.

Jerkhin grabs it out of my hand, and I hear something start—a small engine churning efficiently. He pulls me behind and looks out from the safety of the tree. The pale green lights are getting closer, bobbing with efficiency toward the place where we hide. Jerkhin holds the device out like a wand. He flicks it, and there's a flash of light and then a zap and a space in the woods as if it's on fire. The green lights have retreated, and Jerkhin does it again—flick, zap, flash, fire.

"What are you…" I say, but before I can get the rest of the sentence out, there's a flash above me and a quick buzz, and the tree under which we've been standing, is gone, disappeared. There's a smell like burning newspapers, but that's all that remains. Before I can get a word out, Jerkhin has pulled me behind another tree. He flicks the wand into the distance—zap, flash, fire. In front of us, a flash and a buzz and there's a hole in the ground ten feet by ten feet.

Jerkhin backs up, and I back up with him. We move steadily through the forest. I notice his fingers, his arms, even the muscles in his face are twitching. I haven't been given any weapons. I've been given a backpack and a brassiere and lousy bangs and a Spotify account. I will certainly take this up with my superiors.

Another sound mixes in with the crackling of the fires and Jerkhin's wheeze and the crunch of our feet through the brush. Sirens. I see them now, through the thicket of the woods, red-and-blue flashing getting closer.

The pale green lights suddenly disappear. There's a different kind of whoosh, something up above the tree line moving fast, and I know that whoever was pursuing us is gone.

Jerkhin leans against a tree. He points in the opposite direction from the sirens. "Leads…to…the mall," he says. "Not far."

I turn and then notice that he hasn't moved. "Not without you," I say.

He looks at me, and I see it again, the sadness and resignation.

"Not without you," I say again. I take a step toward him so I'm standing over him, an Earth move that I wouldn't think would work on a Makkelian, or even an Earthling of his size, but my training is taking over. "You haven't been honest with me. You have much to tell me. First of all, who was just trying to kill us?"

He smiles and shakes his head. He holds up a twitching hand for me to help him up. "Meet your. Reptilian. Neighbors," he says.

MISSION REPORT:

QUARTERLY MENTAL HEALTH CHECK-IN

From: Terranaut 6.54.C, Outpost 3429-E, Orion-Cygnus Arm
To: Colonel Muckinzee, Outpost NGC-6946, Fireworks Galaxy

OVERVIEW:

Following, as per protocol, is a quarterly mental-health check-in report from agent Deerdra Grey. Please note that due to the timing of this report, the data enclosed may be sub-optimal. Or it may be optimal. It kind of depends on your definition of optimal, but this agent will, as has been assigned, simply fill out the form to the best of her ability and leave the data analysis to the data analysts.

REPORT TIMING AND MISSION

This report is being filed because it is due, and this agent is in the habit of doing the work assigned to her when it is assigned and toward the best possible outcome, whether she has been given all necessary and relevant information or not. This report is being filed honestly as requested by Minister in Charge of Fitting In, Colonel Ruperto Muckinzee, who stressed the need for candor in filing these reports in all our training exercises.

The agent will go so far as to repeat the words of the Colonel, which have stayed with her since the early days of training. In explaining how important honesty was on mental-health self-diagnostic, stressing that the data collected would be analyzed and then fed back into the very training materials we were studying every day, the materials that formed the bulk of our preparation for this important and dangerous mission, the Colonel said simply: "Clear eyes, full hearts, can't lose."

With clear eyes and a full heart, this agent heretofore indicates that she understands fully that this report is not a gauge of her success or failure or the success or failure of the Federation and its officers to provide her with the very basic tools that might secure her ability to carry out this mission or even to remain safe while doing something as simple as meeting a source for soft serve ice cream. Agent recognizes the importance of this data but also feels the need to point out the subjective nature of her answers to these questions. The agent did not have the best day. The agent has her reasons. The agent's full report is included below.

==

As instructed, agent is using the standard form XR112-3322 Short. All questions are answered below.

1. Do you find it difficult to unwind, relax, or sit still?

Yes. Sometimes.

2. Have you felt irritable and easily annoyed?

Yes. Sometimes. I mean, what kind of question is this? Of course, I have felt irritable and easily annoyed. I have been living under an assumed identity on a small, angry planet. I have been wearing a biosuit that replicates the unlikely biological arrangement of Earth beings, a sack of meat stuffed in a thin layer of skin. I have been wearing Earth clothes proper for my age and gender. I have been assigned a mission that has put me in close contact with American Teenagers, whose behavior is so mystifying, so confounding and strange and illogical and loyal and endearing that I have literally no idea what to think from one minute to the next. Is this person annoying? Funny? Strange? The best? All of the above. Am I this person's friend? Classmate? Contact? Overseer? Their biological and intellectual better? Yes, sometimes I feel irritable and easily annoyed.

3. Have you experienced any issues with your sympathetic nervous system that could be attributed to psychological issues?

Stomach problems, shortness of breath, strong urges to crawl into small spaces? Yes. Sometimes. All the time? The SNS is, as far as I can tell from its automatically generated readouts and reports, performing perfectly. As I have committed to full honesty here, let me say first that it is a feat of engineering. It is a miracle. It has provided perfect cover, and I have never experienced any issues with the performance of the biosuit. However, the suit is perhaps too effective? Perhaps it is worth considering a return to version 4.56, commonly referred to among terranauts as "the version before they figured out the SNS/mind combination." I believe the SNS works perfectly. As a result, I have experienced nothing but psychological issues, stomach problems, shortness of breath, strong urges to do all kinds of things.

4. Have you felt panicked or overwhelmed in either mission situations or your home life?

I feel this way all the time. I feel this way right now. I feel this way more at home than when I am on missions, and now this question has caused me to consider whether that is an unusual situation. This question has caused me to wonder what is wrong with me. This question has caused me to wonder if I am showing proper attention to the chain of command, whether I am becoming too attached to my Earth contacts, whether I am still doing this for the Right Reasons. Yes.

5. Have you had any dreams about our home planet?

No.

Chapter 37
You Are Disrespecting Logan!

Stefanie turns up the television and edges her chair closer. She sips at her wine, places the two weapons—hers and the one they will give to Deerdra tonight—on the coffee table. Onscreen, several women sit around a table. Each of them has a wineglass in front of her. Their faces and hair look almost like the faces and hair of the women in the magazines, or the young women in the documentation movies and television shows, but there's something slightly off about them: their eyes are pinched, they're skintight and shiny and tanned, their hair's perfect but less shiny. Stefanie has wondered before if they are also agents, if their biosuits are better or worse than hers.

She knows about the janitor, the poor ridiculous agent the Makkelians sent and never retrieved, and now he's fumbling around, leaving entire sections of his suit for anybody to find. Thankfully, she and William were able to retrieve that little piece of evidence before any of the MUFON people could show up. Or local law enforcement. Or federal.

The women are becoming excited, a blonde one who's clearly what Deerdra would refer to as "a Popular," stands over a brunette. She holds a wineglass in one hand and points with the other, shouting something about disrespecting somebody named Logan.

Stefanie stands and attempts to mirror the position. She holds the wineglass, leans forward, points a finger, and shouts, "You have been disrespectful to Logan!" at the television. She could do this if it was required. They had anticipated more group social work in this mission—the previous terranauts had spent significant time at things called "get-togethers" and "potlucks." Her father used to mention "fondue parties." She wonders if their lack of socialization will be regarded as a failure. The real estate agent clearly mentioned that the layout of their house would be excellent for entertaining. But every mission is different, she reminds herself, every day on this planet unpredictable and capricious, and the only way to approach a mission is to keep this baseline situation in mind.

She picks up the weapon for Deerdra, a Triumph B she trained with lightly in their preparations. It's fashioned to look like a fidget toy, but they'll have to revamp the styling. It's already feeling dated. What happened last night—Deerdra in a firefight with the Reptilians and nobody around to protect her other than a failing Makkel—for goodness' sake. Unacceptable. They have overridden Colonel Muckinzee in this decision to arm Deerdra, but that leaves her only slightly nervous. The Colonel won't come to Earth until he knows it will be safe to do so. The Greys are here now, and so are the Reptilians. Her first allegiance is to her daughter.

The women on the television are hugging now. Typical Earth people—shouting and pointing one minute and hugging the next. It will be better, she thinks, when they are eradicated and this promising and not yet ruined planet will be theirs alone.

She hears steps on the porch and pauses. Was that a face in the window, peeking through the gap in the thick drapes? Stefanie moves quickly, placing Deerdra's Triumph in a kitchen drawer, her own ready in the back pocket of her jeans.

The doorbell.

She reviews her training for guest protocol: smile, open door, greet the guest, remember to remain smiling. The Real Housewives are excellent role models in some ways.

She moves to the door, one hand on the weapon.

It's the interloper known as "Mrs. V." They've enjoyed a long respite from her unannounced and loud visits, but that streak is apparently broken.

"Hellooooo!" Mrs. V shouts, sailing into the room. Before Stefanie can even close the door, the woman is shouting something else from the kitchen.

"Hello!" Stefanie shouts herself. She can hear the pinched stress in her voice, wonders how Mrs. V is able to be so unabashedly loud.

Mrs. V has poured herself a glass of wine and sits at the table. Stefanie follows suit. She wonders what the blonde Real Housewife would be doing in this situation. She considers shouting, "You have been disrespectful to Logan!" She sits down.

"I just said to myself," Mrs. V says. "It's been just too long since you had a chitchat with your dear friend Stefanie. Is Deerdra home? William?"

Stefanie shakes her head, takes a sip of wine. "School. Work."

Mrs. V pulls her chair closer and puts a hand over Stefanie's hand. This is a move she's seen the Real Housewives do to one another, an effective manner to establish dominance through the appearance of empathy. They think they're so complicated. "It's about Deerdra," Mrs. V says.

"Deerdra?"

"I don't know how to say this, so I'm just going to go ahead and say it: she's been hanging out with a rather...unsavory element."

"Unsavory?" Stefanie pulls her chair closer and is pleased when the tan woman pulls back an inch. "How so?" Mrs. V could pass for one of the housewives, Stefanie realizes, with her face pulled just slightly too tight, her hair styled into light curls every color of yellow.

"It really isn't my... Okay, because we're such good friends. I'll tell you, but it's not pretty." The corners of her mouth and eyes curl up at this. She seems so delighted to deliver bad news. Is Stefanie missing something?

"I am very interested to hear this report," Stefanie says. She pulls even closer. She wonders what would happen if she stood up, held her wineglass in one hand, and pointed with the other and shouted, "You have been disrespectful to Logan!" To Deerdra. To me.

"Well, she's been hanging around with these two kids who are, well, one is Gavin Neary, and I don't have to tell you what his father did last year."

Stefanie stands, pauses for a moment, and watches the woman retreat farther. She retrieves the wine bottle and refills their glasses. "What did he do?"

"Oh goodness me, that's right, you only just moved here. Well, as you know, he's a State Senator, so a very important person around here, of course. Long story short, he had an affair, but it was an affair, well...with someone undesirable. Below his station, for sure. Not the typical little blonde intern."

"Oh."

"Right? A painter or writer or something, some kind of, you know, bohemian. Can you believe that? A senator!"

"And that is all?" Stefanie says. She really needs to move along with her day. There are calculations to be analyzed, news of another crop circle somewhere in Minnesota. There are plans to be made.

"Oh no, honey," Mrs. V says. She pulls her chair in and smooths her hair. "There's this janitor," she says.

"Janitor?" Stefanie says. She takes another sip of wine and feels a wave of exhaustion wash through her. This is becoming tiresome. A month ago, she was so overwhelmed with the social component of their mission, she would have cowered and nodded her head and written the word "janitor" down on a post-it note. Today, she's eager to return to the mission. There is much to be done. And she owes the poor Makkel a debt of gratitude as it turns out. An unfortunate and even embarrassing state of affairs that they will correct this evening.

"I know," Mrs. V says. "I'm afraid it is rather sordid, dear."

Sordid. That's enough. Stefanie stands, feels for the Triumph in her pocket. She has really learned a lot from the Housewives. "Well, this is all just really interesting, but I'm afraid William will be home soon, and Deerdra should be…"

"I'm not done, dear," Mrs. V says. "I suggest you take your hand off that Triumph and sit back down so we can talk this out." She places her own weapon on the table. Stefanie has seen them in pictures and her own training materials, but she had hoped to never come this close to a Reptilian Dokkon.

Stefanie pauses. She regards Mrs. V. "Are all the Real Housewives also Reptilians?" she asks.

"The Orange County ones. The rest are…I don't know, imitating?" Mrs. V says. "Gonna need you to hand that weapon over, honey," she says. Stefanie complies, her eyes on the Dokkon in Mrs. V's hand. One ounce of pressure and Stefanie will simply no longer exist, will be nothing more than a puddle in the seat.

"Sooooo glad we're having this talk!" Mrs. V purrs. Stefanie looks toward the doorway. "Oh, he won't be here in time, honey." She looks at her cell phone. "Stuck in a meeting." She holds up the phone. "Good technology for what it is, right? So adorable how they use them, isn't it, with their little tribes? But soon, we'll be done with all that finally."

"That far along then?" Stefanie says.

"Oh, you know the deal," Mrs. V says. "But you have proven to be worthy adversaries! Or at least, you have proven to be adversaries. More than I can say for that poor janitor and his rudimentary body suit."

"Makkels," Stefanie whispers and shakes her head.

"Indeed," Mrs. V says, scrunching up her face in disgust. "Hard to believe they could even get somebody here to abandon, am I right?"

Stefanie nods. She wonders what the blonde housewife would do in this situation. She's certainly being disrespected. But she looks at Mrs. V again. She is the spitting image of the blonde housewife.

"His people just abandoned him. Typical. But Antheans? Antheans are Council members. Perhaps inferior. Oh, who am I fooling?" Mrs. V says with a smile. "Certainly inferior but still evolved. We are most hopeful that the Council will arrive at a decision that allows you to live happily…I don't know. Somewhere else?" She picks up the Dokkon, clicks it to a setting. "So sorry for you Antheans, having to start all over again on some other planet, and this one just sitting here all blue and ripe for the picking, but—what do they say here on Earth again?—that's just how the cookie crumbles." Stefanie can hear the machine whirring. "See you later, dear," Mrs. V says.

Stefanie hears a soft click, sees a flash, and everything goes black.

Chapter 38
You Think Deerdra is the Only One?

I always liked the term "getting one's hands dirty." Sitting on the sterile ship, reading manuals, and running through digital simulations, the idea of actual dirt and unpredictability was so appealing. I never thought getting my hands dirty would mean they'd be covered in barbeque potato-chip seasoning in Gavin's basement.

Barb lounges on a couch that would have been fashionable five years ago. She flips through Gavin's father's watchlist on the TV. "Spy drama. Courtroom drama. Military drama. Spy drama. Gavin, this explains so much about so many things! It's all drama and covert action around here, isn't it?"

I gulp back a giggle. Little does she know.

Gavin is pacing around, fiddling with a foosball table that looks brand new. You can tell his parents set this basement up with optimistic plans when Gav was still a tween. Gavin would have friends over, and everyone would lounge on the couches and watch TV and play foosball. They'd come upstairs and make build-your-own pizzas in the double decker oven. The girls would trust Gavin's mom with their mild secrets, maybe even confide in her eventually. When they were in college, Gavin and the boys would sneak a beer with his dad. They were going to be the cool house.

But somewhere along the line, that plan clearly didn't work out. The basement is clean, but you can see the disturbances in the dust when you set your soda down on the table, or move one of the two chip bowls, the veggie tray, or the bowl that holds the pizza rolls.

For once, this is the cool house, and Gavin's mom is going all out. I want to tell Mother and Father about pizza rolls. I think they will enjoy them.

"Hey, no spins." Two pairs of legs come down the stairs. "That's illegal." Kayla is here, with Gavin's mom following. They're both carrying food. His mother beams.

"Gavin, you didn't tell me Kayla was coming! First the sweet new girl and now Kayla!"

"Always a pleasure to be an honored guest in your home!" Barb tilts her chin and blinks like a charming Southern belle.

Gavin's mother rolls her eyes. "Always a pleasure to have you, Barbara."

"Mom, I think we have enough food. Do you mind leaving us alone? This Science project is due tomorrow…"

"Sure! Of course! You let me know if you need anything, okay? Kayla? Do you need anything? If you get cold or anything, just say the word. I have sweatshirts you can borrow."

"Yes, thank you, Mrs. Neary. It's so nice of you to have me."

We watch her go back upstairs, wait for the door to click closed.

"Okay, losers, we're really going to be a happy mystery-solving family? Then let's get solving." Barb pulls out her copy of the file. It's covered in pink and yellow highlighter, with tape flags hanging off of random pages. "I think I win the Hermione Award on this one."

Kayla sits on the floor next to Barb. She riffs through a few pages. "Wow. This is…thorough."

"Dates. Names. Places." Barb pushes up her glasses. Thick, black horn rims today. No lenses. "I hate to say it, but I think Eunice was involved with drugs. She liked growing things. She was checking on all of these remote spots everywhere. Pretty clear. Eunice Tiffany: weed kingpin."

She slaps the binder closed, and we stare at each other for a second.

And then Kayla laughs.

"What?!?!" Barb bristles. "I know! She seemed too nice for this. But she must have lied to you. Look at the file. The NSA is erasing things! I'm sorry, Kayla, but you're going to have to face it sometime. Eunice wasn't some sweet, innocent girl from Indiana."

Kayla snorts. "No, she was not. She definitely was not. You think Deerdra's the only one?"

"Kayla!" Gavin finally stops pacing around the edges of the room. He walks to me, grabs my hand, and pulls me down to sit on the floor on Barb's other side. "Um…" he says.

"Oh." To her credit, Kayla's laugh instantly disappears and concern washes over her face. "Oh no, I'm so sorry."

Barb fidgets on the couch. "What's going on?" she says.

Gavin reaches over and grabs her hand, too. The three of us, connected again. "Deerdra? Gav? You know I love a lovefest, but this is weird."

I take a deep breath. Sympathetic nervous system activated. Gavin squeezes my hand. I wonder if he can feel it shaking.

"Okay. Remember when we were hiding from Jerkhin in the equipment room, and you said writing 'How I Solved a Murder' would make for a good admissions essay someday? Well, what if it was…bigger than that?"

"I just said it was bigger than that. Oh my God, are you in on whatever Eunice was up to?"

"No. Well, yes. But I didn't know it until recently. Barb. Um. I'm not from here."

"Yeah, you're from New Mexico. You were homeschooled. You are new. You told everyone. You were like a robot. Oh my God, are you a robot? Is your mission to exterminate?" Barb uses a robot voice for this last line, all in good fun. I freeze.

"Hey, Deerdra?" Kayla leans in a little. "Can I help? Eunice and I had a talk like this, and it took a long time for us to have our breakthrough. But when it clicked, it clicked."

"Yes!" I'm so relieved. Kayla has done this before. Kayla will be able to help. She understands how people work. She will be able to guide Barb's brain through this process.

"Excellent. Barb, you can be cool, right? I'm going to do a thing, and you're going to remember to be cool."

Barb nods.

"Good. Take this." She hands Barb a throw pillow and moves behind me, puts a hand on my shoulder. "When Deerdra says she's not from here, she's really…like really, really not from here." And with that, she reaches up and pulls my hair, hard. It holds for the first second but then comes off in one smooth piece.

Barb's mouth drops open at the sight of the wig in Kayla's hand. And then she looks up and sees my smooth, bald, grey head and the tops of my black eyes. She gasps.

"Nope. Nope nope nope."

Kayla holds the throw pillow. "If you're going to scream, scream into this."

It takes a while to get Barb to calm down, but all things considered, she handles it well. Maybe her time in drama club is paying off. She throws herself into someone else's story three times a year—an alien girl playing human is just a level up from there.

Barb and Kayla drop their fight for a while. They're two girls from Indiana who both had alien friends. Their differences seem pretty small now.

We lie on the floor with our heads together in the dim room and talk about what we all know. Things start to become clear.

Eunice and Kayla became friends thanks to a combination of luck and the alphabet—their last names were close enough that they sat near each other in a number of classes, and teachers tended to pair the quiet new girl up with popular Kayla to try to get Eunice out of her shell.

"She was smarter than everyone else in the room, so we'd always finish our partner activities before everyone else. And then we'd just…talk. She really was one of the kindest people ever, and she knew a little something about anything and everything, so she was always, I don't know, just like really interesting to talk to."

Colonel Muckinzee, or whoever prepared Eunice's mission, would be proud to hear this.

"But she wasn't just interesting—she was *interested*. I could tell her that I got an A in Chemistry, or that I feel bad for earthworms on the sidewalk after it rains, or that I've always been afraid of my grandma's doll collection. I'd tell her anything, and she'd want to learn more and she'd never judge. It's so hard to find someone who lets you be yourself."

Barb grimaces, probably remembering a thousand little digs she threw at Kayla, at others. "So how did you find out she wasn't from here?"

Kayla reaches over and fiddles with a tress of my hair for a minute. We put the wig back in place right after the big reveal. It was a good way to explain things to Barb, but I don't think Gavin's mother would bounce back as fast.

"Deerdra, do you ever have to recharge? Breathe a different atmosphere for a while?"

"Yes. My parents' rec room looks a little different than this. If we don't rejuvenate, things—my biosuit?—starts to degrade and my brain gets a little foggy."

Barb rubs between her eyebrows. "You guys, this is the weirdest day I'm ever going to have in my life. I was doing fine, but 'biosuit' is kind of bringing it all back."

"My outfit?"

"Better."

Kayla says, "About a year before she disappeared, Eunice got obsessed with those missions of hers. She really would wake up before dawn and bike around the county. One day, she hit a rut and went flying off her bike. She was already pushing the limits on how long she could…wear her outfit…without dry-cleaning it?"

Barb nods and whispers, "Better."

"She broke her bike and ripped her outfit. She was stuck outside for most of the day, trying to walk back without being seen. She waited until dark and then called me to come and pick her up. She definitely had that brain fog going—she saw me and gave me a huge hug and said she was so glad to see me, and that I was her best friend ever and she wasn't going to let anything ever happen to me."

Kayla's eyes well up a bit. "She seemed like she had been out at a field party or something—just full of love and feeling chatty. But then she started talking about military people who like 80s movies but didn't care about Earth. Which, okay, weird, but we kept driving. And then she started complaining about how she felt like she couldn't even be herself anymore, and how everything was so fake, and she just wanted to escape. And I get that!"

Barb, Gavin, and I all mutter some variant of "yes" at the same time. All four of us smile at each other for just a second.

"So I thought I was being the perfect supportive friend. I was listening and giving her a safe ride home. We got to her place, and it was totally dark, so I helped her inside. You guys…it was so weird in there. Like one of those furniture stores that's set up to look like people live there, but it's all too perfect. She really wasn't doing well at this point. I was thinking I'd set her up in the bathroom and bring her some water and crackers because it looked like she was going to have a rough night. But she insisted that I take her down to the basement."

"Let me guess," I said. "Little room. Locked door. Grey and pink."

"Exactly. And she walks in and takes a deep breath, and then just takes her hair off like you or I would kick off our shoes. That's how I knew to do the pillow thing, Barb. Because I *screamed*."

"Okay, that? Was a baller move," Barb says. "I couldn't even scream anymore because I couldn't seem weak right after such. A. Baller. Move."

"Thanks," Kayla says.

"So new Science project," Barb says, looking at me with what I can tell is legitimately renewed interest. "What other weird, crazy, awesome things can you do?"

Chapter 39
Mom?

"Hey, Mom," I shout up the stairs. "Door was open." Nothing. The car is in the driveway, and there are two half-full glasses of wine sitting on the kitchen table, an empty bottle on the counter. There's a fidget spinner sitting on the table, and I pick it up and spin. Dark blue, some kind of metal. A really good fidget spinner. Heavy—a spin that is straight and true and lasts for longer than a minute. I put it in my pocket and go down to check the home room, but she's not there. She isn't in the bedroom or the bathroom or the yard. Probably, she's taking a walk or is visiting a neighbor—they finished the wine here and went to another house for more provisions. Or some other housewife kind of activity.

I go up to my room. Everything seems to be in order. My parents' room looks the same as always.

"Stefanie, I'm home!" It's Father. Thank goodness. Right now, I need my father and my team leader.

"Hey," I say, coming down the stairs. "She's not here..."

"The car is in the driveway," he says. "Did she leave a note? Is she downstairs?"

"No on both," I say.

"No note would be a serious breach of protocol," he says. And then he's running out the door, and I follow. He opens the trunk and literally breathes a sigh of relief. He leans against the car, and I see two briefcases in the trunk, one regular and one made of some kind of metal.

"Okay," he says. "This is serious but not as serious as it could be." He picks up the metal briefcase.

I take the fidget spinner out of my pocket and give it a spin.

"No!" Father says. He grabs the spinner out of my hand.

"What?" I say. "Give me that back."

He puts the spinner in his pocket and picks up the metal briefcase.

"What's going on?" I say. "Where's Mother? Are we in trouble?"

A woman jogs by with an orange dog on a leash. She slows and stares. "Hello!" Father shouts. "Good afternoon!" We wave and smile, and the woman nods and wanders down the street.

Father leads me inside, and we sit at the coffee table. He takes the two wine glasses and puts them on the counter. "This is not good," he says. "I believe your mother may have been abducted."

"Abducted?" I say. "By who?"

He places the fidget spinner on the table and then drops the briefcase, which lands with a shudder. "Reptilians," he says. "Doggone Reptilians."

Father takes a long time making the hot chocolate—heating the water, opening the little packets, swirling the solution around with a spoon, waiting for it to cool. He keeps checking his communication device, and I believe that he is stalling, waiting for something or somebody. Or maybe he's just not sure what to do without Mother here.

He has taken Level 1 Precautionary Measures: country music blares from the radio in the kitchen; in the living room, blonde, middle-aged women shout at one another from a hot tub. The doors are all locked, windows locked, entire house checked once again for listening devices or unknown radio or Wi-Fi signals. We are alone. Or, as alone as it is possible for us to be in this situation. I stare at Mother's chair, at the two wineglasses on the counter. We are definitely alone.

Finally, he sits down and places a steaming mug in front of me. I remember Jerkhin eating that vanilla soft serve. Chocolate is a thing I will miss, when and if this is over and there's time for missing things. I think about Barb and Gavin and then push the thought out of my mind, focus on the steam swirling out of the mug. The science is obvious—the liquid evaporates and then condenses back into tiny droplets of water that swirl up and around the cup but it's more than just the science. It is also—what is the word? It's lovely. I would not have understood that before this mission. I hope to be able to put this understanding to use in the future.

Father just sits. He takes a drink of his tea. Something in him is stuck. Again I wonder if he's buying time or waiting for instructions or thinking or just...stuck.

"So those doggone Reptilians," I say.

He sighs, and his entire body seems to settle, like a person enjoying the last moment of a lazy morning in bed. "Okay," he says, his voice shifting into Mission Leader mode. "There are some things you need to know about."

"You think?" I say.

"Ha ha," he says, his tone flat and sarcastic.

"You learned sarcasm."

"I have been getting better. And so have you. I noticed. We noticed."

I sit up and pull my chair closer. "Are we evacuating?" I ask. "Is Mother gone?"

"Oh," he says. "Oh no, Deerdra. It is actually the exact opposite. If I am reading the situation correctly."

"Which one?"

"Which what?"

"Which opposite, Father? Are we evacuating? Is Mother gone?"

He stands and walks to the sink, stares at the wineglasses. "Well, your mother is gone. She is not here. I do not know where she is but she did not follow the casual documentation protocol so…"

"She didn't leave a note?"

"So, as Mission Leader, I have no option but to consider her abducted."

"By the Reptilians," I say.

"Doggone Reptilians," he says. "Here. On Earth."

"But why?" I say, but as soon as the word "reptilian" hits my ears I understand what it means, that we are not alone, that to the Reptilians we are the Makkel, fumbling around with our backward technology, like cows sent to take over a government building.

"That is what I am saying," he says. "If I am reading the situation correctly, we are not evacuating. In fact, if I am reading this situation correctly, one way or another, we may never again be leaving this planet."

I'm trying to understand. The Reptilians are here. But it doesn't explain Father's last statement. "Why?" I say. "The mission was always to find out what we could find out and then go…I don't know, wherever."

"There may be more to it than you were allowed to know about. Than we thought you should be asked to carry."

"I was looking for Eunice Tiffany. Reptilians?"

"It was one theory. The other was the janitor. The other that she had…gone native?"

"I'll take all of the above for 500, Alex," I say under my breath.

"Currently, the least of our priorities, and while I am interested in your last statement, time is of the essence, and we must move along."

"So, the first of our priorities: finding Mom, then going home?"

"We will find your mother," he says. "I do not believe there would have been evidence left of a visitation without contact coming soon about their specific demands."

"And then we go…" I say, my stomach sinking and voice catching, realizing I have no idea how to end that sentence. Stupid sympathetic nervous system.

"It's just that," he says. "We are never going home. Deerdra." He looks me in the eye, squeezes my hand, and then looks toward the window. "There is no home to go back to."

Chapter 40
Dad!

We're in the basement, in the home room. I'm holding the Triumph Spinner Weapon in both hands, my index fingers closed together over one of the three prongs of what I previously thought was just a really good fidget spinner.

"Press together," Father says. "Keep them pointed at the wall, pointed like a gun. Don't be afraid. Go ahead and press them together and…"

I press my fingers together and feel the machine start to buzz, then a laser bolt is pushing out of the Triumph—it moves quickly but not like a shot, more like a stream of water from a high-powered hose. It fizzles into the wall of the home room, leaves a strange smell of burning chemicals. I remember that smell, catching Mother in here, the way she just retreated back up the stairs and didn't say a word. I wonder what else I haven't been told.

"Try again," Father says. "You can't hurt that wall. This time, try moving your fingers, first side to side very slowly, and then up and down. You will learn to control it."

I press my fingers together, feel the buzz, and the laser is coming out of the Triumph. I move to the left, to the right, and the laser bolt moves in the same direction. I flick, and it breaks, fizzes against the wall, and then starts again.

"Good," Father says. "Try again. You have unlimited ammo. Unlimited energy. Just concentrate."

A knock on the front door. It is muted and distant but it is a knock. We pause, look at one another. Another knock. Father looks at me. He motions toward the stairs. I watch him close up the home room, putting an extra lock that I haven't seen before on the frame. He motions that I should place the Triumph in my pocket, and I follow him up the stairs.

At the front door, he indicates for me to have the Triumph at the ready. A knock and then a sound like somebody crashing against the door.

"They have come already with their terms. I thought it would arrive through…" Father says. "I thought more official channels."

"Actually," I say. "I think I know who this might be." I look through the keyhole and see nothing. I'm not sure if it's a trick of the sympathetic nervous system, but I believe I can smell him through the door: chemicals, sweat, orange juice. "You are not going to like this," I say to Father.

Father looks through the keyhole, and of course, he can see nothing but the neighbor's house, the SUVs lazily moving up and down the streets of our development. I can hear him, wheezing on the ground. Good news that he's still alive.

I open the door, and even I'm shocked at his appearance. He's deflated, coming apart. He looks like the cows after Mother and Father have done their experiments. "Good gravy," Father says. "You bring him here? To our home? At a time like this?"

"We should help him," I say, grabbing an arm.

"A Makkel!" Father whispers as if I'm unsure exactly where the janitor comes from, like this is news to me. I realize I, too, have been keeping secrets.

I grab the right arm, the only one left, and start pulling. "Get him inside," I say. "You can yell at me later, but for now…" I look out at the neighborhood. Two women are power-walking toward us. They are both wearing yoga pants and headphones and are talking over whatever they're listening to. We get Jerkhin inside just as they round the corner.

Father follows the security protocols again, checking the locks on the doors and windows, ensuring that there are no viewpoints through the shades, and runs upstairs. I get Jerkhin seated at the table. He's in worse shape than I've ever seen him; the entire left half of his face has caved in, like somebody kicked a doll's head. Both legs sit at awkward angles as if their connection to the joint is failing. Where the left arm would be, there are frayed tubes and wires, organic-like willow limbs, but tubes and wires nevertheless. I remember hearing about biosuits made in this manner, the precursor to the precursor of my current equipment. I can't believe he's made it this long. I get him a glass of orange juice, and he drinks it, and I watch as the broken cords in the left arm drip orange for a few seconds. He puts his head down on the table and wheezes. "Mrrrphmph…" he says.

"I don't…" I say.

"Will be. Done soon," he says. "They will. Not come." And then rests his head again, as if the effort of saying those few words is all he could expel.

"Who do you mean by they?" I ask.

"My. People." He wheezes. All over his biosuit, a thin layer of green bubbles, like sweat, has started up. He wipes at them and looks at his hand. "Mrrrrrphmph," he says.

"My father is...our Mission Leader will be here soon," I say, looking up toward the top floor where Father is slamming cabinets. "I don't know what I can do after that."

Jerkhin keeps his head down. He reaches into his back pocket, fishes around a bit, and finally plops his hand on the table. I hear Father coming down the stairs. I slip my hand under Jerkhin's massive paw and pull out a hard piece of paper, a postcard, and slip it into my pocket. Jerkhin exhales in a wheeze, and the smell overtakes the room. I stand up and walk toward the window, almost open it, and then realize this would be a major breach of protocol in a Security 1 situation.

Father continues down the stairs, past this level, and into the basement. I hear the freezer open and close.

Jerkhin is still. I put a hand where the heart simulator on his suit would be. Nothing. I put a hand over the mouth. The biosuit and the terranaut inside are both dead.

Father comes up the stairs, carrying something large and long that I can't quite see behind the tears. We don't cry on my planet. I'm experiencing what the Earth people call loss. Jerkhin was my friend? Was he my friend? And now my friend is gone.

Father puts something on the table. "Is he gone?" he says. "They are not a very advanced people. He has been here too long. I thought if he had this back then maybe..." He places Jerkhin's arm on the table. "There are some more things we should talk about," he says.

Chapter 41
Memorial for a Makkel

"He was a…brave man. A brave citizen, terranaut. Even braver, perhaps, as he was a Makkel and therefore just such an inferior…"

"Father!" I say. "I don't think now is the time for that kind of thing."

Father nods. Jerkhin's body is stretched out in front of us, his legs still jutting out at bad angles, his arm laid down by his side. He is even more grey than before and now resembles nothing so much as a rhinoceros in a black janitor's outfit. I remind myself that this is not his real body, that beneath this rough suit, there is a Makkel who bears all the traits—the long fingers, short neck, large, bulbous head, and rough green skin of his people. Maybe he is handsome on his planet. Maybe he had a wife, children, friends who have been waiting for his arrival, waiting for a word, just to know that he is safe.

"He loved vanilla soft serve ice cream," I say. "He was trying to help Eunice Tiffany."

Father jolts and looks at me.

"You are not the only one who's been keeping secrets," I say.

He nods, and I can't tell if he is mad or impressed or both, can't tell whether he is my Father or my Mission Leader. I realize how much I don't know about everything. He tightens his black tie. "We will need to review plans from here. Procedure. It is important. This has not gone well, Deerdra. There is much at stake."

"Why?" I say. The door to the home room is held open with a brick, and it looks just like…a room, a normal room.

"Why?" He tightens the tie again, a nervous tick, and his neck becomes pink, the skin pushing out over the border of his collar. "Because I said so, and I am Mission Leader."

"No," I say, aware that I'm breaking protocol but not even caring, "I mean, why is there so much that I don't know? I'm on this mission, as well. I'm a part of this family, this team. I can do things. I can…" I look down and remember that we're supposed to be giving Jerkhin a dignified and appropriate memorial. His left side is evaporating, sinking into itself. He's starting to look less like a large Earth man and more like a melting air mattress. The feeling starts in my throat and moves up into my face, and I'm struggling for breath, my eyes filling with tears.

I think about what's happening to my nervous system, a trick to try to calm it down: my emotions have triggered a fight or flight instinct, which has the side effect of shutting down nonessential resources, which is why my throat has constricted, my breathing is shallow. I listen to the sounds coming from my throat. I take a deep breath and then another. Finally, I rub at the tears and open my eyes.

Father looks terrified. "I am sorry," he says. "We should have been more forthcoming about the mission. About a lot of things."

"Father," I say and dart my eyes at Jerkhin.

"Oh, I am sorry," he says. "Would you like to say anything else?"

I pause and gather my thoughts. I think about him licking that ice cream. "I think he was a good man," I say and then nod at Father.

He adjusts something on his Triumph and motions me to step through the door. I hear a buzz, see a dull glow. When I come back inside, there's only the janitor's uniform. "Wow," I say.

"We'll cover that in another lesson," Father says.

His communication device buzzes, and he walks into a corner, taps at the machine for a while, waits for an answer.

"Okay," he says. "They have set a place."

"For?"

"Either they are going to give us your Mother back, and we will come to an agreement about how to manage the situation—both groups being here—or they will kill us all and take over the Earth."

"Reptilians?"

"Doggone Reptilians."

"But how…why do you think they would even still have Mother? Why not just proceed to step two and take over Earth?"

"There is a protocol."

"Protocol?"

"The Council. The Intergalactic Advanced Species Homestead Protocol."

"That's the protocol you're talking about? Father, Reptilians don't pay any attention to that. They wipe out planets and bury their eggs in the ground and bam, more Reptilians. They will evaporate us as soon as they would say hello to us on the street. They were shooting at me and Jerkhin just the other night. They almost killed us."

"Almost," he says. "Think about that. You think they couldn't have killed your poor friend here? You think they wouldn't have taken his arm?"

I have to stop and think. "Why didn't they kill us, then? Why didn't they take his arm?"

"Because your mother and I took his arm."

"You…"

"We have not left you completely on your own," he says.

Always, more questions.

Father puts his arm around me. "Your friend Gavin called the fire department. A smart boy, that one."

"But then why didn't they just kill us? Me and…" I point to the janitor's uniform, greasy and wrinkled on the floor.

"That is what I am saying." Father's voice is quiet, calm, the voice he used to use when reading me a bedtime story. "The Reptilians will think nothing of killing a Makkel but an Anthean is different. We are Council members. There are protocols."

"Protocols. Like this call you just got?"

"That is a part of it, yes. Without rules, Deerdra, everything would just be…"

"Chaos."

Father nods. "Chaos," he says. "And Reptilians, well, they are just not a chaotic species. They are very advanced, remember, even more than us. They are smart and careful. Smart and careful enough to understand fully that there is no highside…highside?"

"Upside."

"No upside to the humans finding out early. They are very careful about maintaining the sanctity of their mission until it is time."

"Time to wipe out a planet and literally sow their own seeds."

"That time. Yes."

Father's device buzzes again, and he nods. "We need to go," he says. "Can you bring your mother a sweater?"

"A sweater?" I cannot believe he would be thinking about a sweater right now. "Is that some kind of code or something? Some other protocol?"

He shakes his head. He squeezes my arm and smiles. "It is cold," he says. "She may be chilly."

Report:

The Intergalactic Advanced Species Homestead Protocol
by Deerdra Grey, Terranaut in Training

Developed by the First Council of Advanced Species, the Intergalactic Advanced Species Protocol provides guidelines for interstellar travel and annexation by higher forms of life. In our peoples' case, it took seven generations of council members to finalize the protocol. (The varying lifespan length among advanced species caused many headaches. For example, the delegation from Sennario had to leave the council after supplying nearly 600 for the first four extended sessions. While Bustaryme technology is some of the most sophisticated, they were bankrupting their resources trying to provide transit to each new delegate, only to replace them several Anthean weeks later.)

The Intergalactic Advanced Species Protocol is obviously complex and important. In our modern times, with Reptilian influence over the Council steadily increasing and Anthean budgets for interplanetary travel remaining stagnant, the Protocol provides a steadying influence over the complicated issue of planet annexation and exploration.

CRITERIA:

In its wisdom, the Council has created a mathematical equation that factors in all instances in which the protocol is initiated:

____Is said planet a current member of the Council of Advanced Species? (40 points)

____Is more than 20% of biomass on this planet sentient? (10 points)

____Have the sentient beings on this planet discovered nuclear technology? (5 points)

____Are the most advanced life forms on this planet capable of extra-solar communication? (5 points) Off-planet travel? (10 points) Faster-than-light travel? (30 points)

If said planet's score is greater than 70, the Intergalactic Species Protocol dictates that sentient beings on the planet may be contacted and potentially nominated for membership into the Council. Scores between 50-70 show potential for future partnerships. Council members may observe these cultures but not make contact.

Scores of less than 50 show no potential for growth; the planet may be annexed by a participating Council planet.

PROCESSING, APPEALS, AND SPECIAL CIRCUMSTANCES:

Annexation preferences will go in order of paperwork filed with the Council Magistrate; however, waivers received within seven of the annexable planet's business days will be considered by the Magistrate, and rulings will be made following the parameters laid out in the full Intergalactic Advanced Species Protocol.

- "Monopoly" clause: If a member species is a) decidedly more advanced AND b) has filed annexation paperwork on three or more planets within 20 light years of each other, preference may be given to that species regardless of other annexation claims.
- Historians believe this clause was created in the early days of the protocol to encourage the most advanced species to colonize nonmember planets and leave member planets alone. The council hoped to entice the major powers to use their resources to travel to new colonies and end the wars between member planets. The original title and details of this clause take over a terabyte of memory. Instead, we borrowed the new title and concept from an Earth board game: Why fight over Marvin Gardens when one of you can own the utilities and the other the railroads?

INTER-COUNCIL CONDUCT STANDARDS:

A certain standard of decorum is expected among council members. The universe is nearly infinite: why kill other advanced species when there are so few of us and so many inferiors?

Exceptions to this rule include self-defense, failure to adhere to the terms of the Advanced Species Homesteading Protocol, and when a loss of life can be proven to have a positive overall impact on the greater good.

PROTOCOL USAGE:

Because of the extreme nature of the Protocol and advanced security around all Council records, it is impossible to determine how many times the Protocol has been utilized. In an interview for the Anthean Columnustrate, Chief Counsel in

Charge Leeonel Phyphe indicated that interplanetary annexation claims had been made "more than once and less than a thousand times." Regardless and much to the point, the statement provides no additional context for this report.

FUTURE OF THE PROTOCOL:

In that same interview, Phyphe states that "the future of the Protocol is up to the Reptilians," a statement that seems to have gained consensus among Council representatives. Now, with a majority of Council seats, Reptilians have the capacity to repeal the Protocol altogether, create new protocols, or simply vote in favor of Reptilia in any and all annexation claims. The future of planet annexation, it appears, is quite Reptilian.

Chapter 42
Three to Five Earth Business Days

We pull into the place, and Father stops the car while we survey the situation. In front of us and to the left is a small hexagonal restaurant. Women on roller skates move in and out, carrying trays of cheeseburgers, fries, sodas, and ice cream. Through the steamed windows, we can see three figures at work, moving rapidly, flipping and frying and arranging food that is then shoved through a window for delivery by a roller-skating waitress.

I remember places like this from the documents, the older ones from the period known as "The Fifties." I will never understand how these people experience such intense nostalgia for a period that has only just happened. Sixty, seventy Earth years? It is a blip, a pause, a cough to the universe. They are silly beings, but I've grown fond of some of them.

The parking lot is crowded with cars, most of them with their windows down, trays lodged aside their passenger doors. Entire families have chosen to eat their dinner in the crowded confines of their automobiles.

"They are the strangest beings," Father says. "Just really barely even sentient. They have invented a massive wireless network that connects nearly every living being, traveled into space, although only to their own moon which is just embarrassing, they fancy themselves poets and scientists, and this is how they choose to spend their evenings. Just…anyway, let's see about some soft serve here."

In the back, in the very corner of the row of picnic tables that extends from the gravelly parking lot toward a weedy field in the distance, sits Mrs. V. She waves and smiles, takes a sip from a milkshake. She's dressed in a black, sleeveless dress as if she has stopped on her way to a cocktail party. She's tan and blonde and looks just like the ladies on Mother's Real Housewives shows. Her arms are thin and muscular. Of course, I think, she is a Reptilian. I can't believe I didn't notice this before. There's so much that's slipped right past me.

There are two men with her, both dressed in black suits with ties and black hats. They're each attending to ice cream cones, soft serve, vanilla. It really is the favorite of the out-of-town crowd, I think. "I'm going to miss this," Jerkhin had said.

I don't see my mother.

I expected to be scared, but instead, my sympathetic nervous system delivers the symptoms associated with anger. I feel the Triumph spinner in my pocket.

Father parks and we get out of the car. I want to run at her, to spin a beam right at their stupid soft serve.

"Deerdra," Father says. I look to him and can see he's thinking, fumbling for the right phrase. "Be cold," he says.

"Be cool, Father," I say. "You mean, be cool."

Mrs. V waves us toward their table. The two men just eat their ice cream. Father holds up a finger and walks toward the place where people are waiting in line. "Father?" I say. "Shouldn't we…."

"We should retain protocol," he says. "Fit in. Especially in a meeting with, well, others. It is even more important that we all be seen as fitting in. All of us. Us and them. In a public place."

I can tell by the way he says "public" that he doesn't feel the meeting place has been well chosen. Like all advanced species, of course, we have great respect for and even greater fear of the Reptilians. They are capricious and aggressive colonists. Their sense of ethics doesn't extend beyond their own species. They are physically overpowering and technically advanced. In our training, we were educated on Reptilians, of course—they have always been the greatest threat to any other species. Or the greatest threat other than us, because it's not the Reptilians' fault that we're on this mission, that our planet has become uninhabitable. I understand all of this. What I don't understand is why they haven't killed us yet.

Father orders two vanilla soft serves, and I follow him to the table. My mind is reeling, and I feel like I'm floating, like all of this is happening in a dream, as if there's a great distance between my head and my feet scraping along the gravel, getting closer to the Reptilians who have taken my mother, who tried to evaporate me and Jerkhin, who may have taken Eunice Tiffany.

Eunice Tiffany. So this is what all of that was about? The Reptilians weren't really worried about actually finding the missing terranaut. They were doing a threat assessment, trying to find out if there were any other species looking to colonize Earth. And they were doing that threat assessment through me. And I pulled in Barb and Gavin and Kayla. I pulled Jerkhin back in. I have put everybody in danger and for what? To inform a white paper that will be delivered to the colonels and the generals and the congress, hovering light years above our dying planet? For a policy decision to be made and handed down while Mother quite literally wastes away on a Reptilian prison ship? For a few powerful planets who already have too much to gain even more, no matter who it hurts? Or kills?

I've been an idiot. Worse, I've been exactly what they wanted me to be.

"Well, hi there, girly!" Mrs. V says. She stands and hugs me, and I'm transported to the here and now, the gravel under my feet, Mrs. V's perfume smell, her hands squeezing my back. She ends the hug and pulls back, looks me up and down. My sympathetic nervous system churns contradictory chemicals through my biosuit. I'm angry and sad and embarrassed and fighting the urge to hug Mrs. V back, to sit in her lap and ask if she will gently pet my hair.

"You never did figure out how to do your hair on your own, did you, sweetie?" she says.

The two men stand and introduce themselves to Father as Mr. A and Mr. L.

"Good afternoon," Father says. He licks at his soft serve, and I do the same. It really is delicious. I wonder if Jerkhin's people will ever know what happened to him. He really did love soft serve ice cream.

"So Stefanie is fine," Mrs. V says. She sounds like a doctor giving positive test results. "She will be kept quite comfortable while everything gets worked out."

"Worked out?" Father says.

"Yepper," Mrs. V says. "The Council. Our people are talking to your people, as dictated by the Homestead Protocol. As we are the more advanced species, it is incumbent upon us to deliver a proposal for homestead here, and we will do that in…" she turns to Mr. A.

"Three to five Earth business days," he says.

"Three to five Earth business days!" Mrs. V says. "So in the meantime, we'll keep good care of…"

"No!" I say. "No, that's not okay. None of this is okay." Tears are welling up in my eyes. I stand up, and Mr. A stands, as well. He reaches for something in his jacket pocket, and Mrs. V pats him on the arm. He sits back down. "Three to five days to find out if I'm going to get my mother back. That's not okay. A bunch of generals bartering a planet. A planet! Like they're trading uranium. There are people here. Millions of them."

"Deerdra," Father says. "You know these people are not advanced."

"But they are! They might be younger than us, less civilized, less technologically advanced."

Father's face changes from a look of concern to anger. Now I'm team member who's jeopardizing his mission. "Deerdra, let's go," Father says. He turns to Mrs. V and nods. "We will see you in three to five Earth business days."

"They might be less advanced than us, but they're funny, and complicated, and sad and happy and weird!"

"Oh my goodness," Mrs. V says. She's smiling and shaking her head. "Look who's gone native."

Father grasps my elbow.

"We are leaving," he says.

"Hold on," Mrs. V says. "So we're clear." She points to me. "So we're clear with me and you." She isn't smiling anymore. "We will wait three to five business days, and we will see what our generals say, and when the word comes down that Earth is to be a Reptilian zone, then you will leave or die like the rest of these Earth cows, and our advanced species won't think about you or your mission or your janitor or your little friends ever again. We will plant our seeds and poison the atmosphere and when we rise, as we should, there won't be so much as a gross earthling bone remaining on this planet. We will do it because we are advanced. We are stronger. We will take what we deserve. Are we clear?"

I want to say something cutting and cool, something Barb would say, but all I do is shake my head. "Yes," I say.

Chapter 43
Don't You Try and Pretend

We don't talk much on the car ride home. Father turns the radio to his country station. I look out the window.

"That was not advisable," he says.

"I know," I say.

He dials up the volume on the radio. A lonesome-sounding man sings about how all his exes live in Texas. It's plainly clear that he arrived at the rhyme first and then lyrics later, that he created an entire song around the rhythmic similarity of the words "exes" and Texas, two words that are only two letters apart. I feel even more ridiculous for defending this ridiculous planet.

The buildings and the cars and people roll by in the window. The car. Another ridiculous practice, driving a machine that weighs four thousand pounds on roads made of asphalt and gravel and wheels made of rubber. On the ground. They are a ridiculous species, but it is nice and melancholy how the buildings slide by and the man on the radio sings in a syncopated ache, and I feel like the teenagers in the documents, sad and beautiful and none of it is my fault. Or all of it is my fault. I don't know. Maybe that's part of the equation, part of what brings the tears to my eyes even as the tendril of anger remains twitching in my fingertips. I wish I had thought of the right thing to say. I wish I had pulled out my Triumph and held it to her stringy, tanned neck, demanded that they release my mother in three to five Earth business minutes. Would that have been, what is the word Barb would use? Badass?

We pull into our development, and Father turns the radio down. He is so careful, such a rule follower. Can't have any of the neighbors hearing what we're listening to inside the privacy of our Camry. Can't push the generals to release his wife and team member. Can't push Mrs. V or the Council. "Typical," I whisper under my breath.

Father stops the car in our driveway. "Excuse me?" he says.

"I said typical. Typical. It means ordinary. It means, same as it ever was. It means someone or something has failed me in a way that meets a pre-established pattern."

Father just sighs. "This is how it works," he says, "the protocol…"

"I know," I say, unbuckling my seatbelt. "Typical."

I leave him there, double-checking his briefcases, and move into the house. The security protocols are in place, of course, and I take care to turn them off, to sweep the house for intruders and then for listening or radio devices. I go into the kitchen and pour myself a glass of orange juice. I pause and look at those two wineglasses, the empty bottle sitting on the counter. There was a time when I wondered why we weren't gathering DNA from that second glass, the one with the bright pink lipstick. But now I know. Now I know they knew all along that Mrs. V was a Reptilian. They knew, and they sent me into high school to investigate the mystery of Eunice Tiffany anyway. I was never Hermione. I was never even Ron Weasley. I was always Neville Longbottom, fumbling around, getting my friends ever closer to real danger.

Finally, I go into my room. I put on the soundtrack from one of my favorite documents. I didn't understand the way the teenagers in the documents were so melancholy. I didn't understand how they could be so happy one moment and then sad. So dramatic. So tragic and all for nothing, for boys or girls or proms or parents that just don't understand. They are so silly, with their clothes and their foosball tables and jokes and hugs.

"Don't you forget about me," the singer sings. It's all so silly and dramatic, and the tears come down, and it feels bad and good, and finally I understand.

I understand. I know what I need to do.

Chapter 44
Is This Real?

I need to get in touch with Barb and Gavin—and Kayla—so weird how all this has happened—if this is all going to work. I will need to think about what it will mean for this to work, what it will mean for later, after, for Mother and Father and the rest of our dying planet. Our dead planet.

But is that the point, now, anyway? It was the point, the entire point of this mission. Now I know that. Or I think I do. All that I've learned in the past forty-eight hours is everything they didn't tell me. Not even everything because I'm positive there's more. All I really know is I shouldn't have trusted them in the first place. Mother and Father and Colonel Muckinzee and all of them have deceived me, patronized me like a rabbit, in a way that Barb, Gavin, Kayla, and even Jerkhin, with his one arm and his wheezing and his soft serve, never would. Jerkhin who is a stain on the floor of our home room right now.

I wonder if they are even my parents, if our shared history is a real memory, or if it has been implanted in order to better facilitate the impression that we're indeed a family unit. I don't want to be thinking this. I've heard about it before—whispers, dark insinuations—but I've never allowed myself to really ask the question.

What do I know for sure? What have I learned in the past few days? The Reptilians are here. Father and Mother have been doing much of the same work as Eunice Tiffany: collecting samples, trying to identify areas where the Reptilians have nested, are nesting, are likely to nest. Mrs. V is a Reptilian. The Real Housewives of Orange County, as well, although I probably would have guessed that before. They have taken Mother. They had me looking for Eunice Tiffany, not because they were concerned for her welfare, but as a kind of canary in the coalmine, as they say. They were looking for a hint, a clue, an assessment of who else was here and what information the generals would need to sift through in order to determine which species got to wipe all life off of this planet and colonize it as their own.

What else? Gavin is a good friend. Gavin has a foosball table. Barb is funny and mean and tough. Kayla is more like Barb than either of them would ever admit. Earth friends are a less advanced but complicated species. They will surprise you. They will make you laugh. They will make you furious and confused, and even after you tell them you're an alien from a planet they couldn't remotely imagine, they can still make you feel wanted and loved and respected. They can make you feel like you belong even if there's no way in any universe that it should be true.

I remember a breakfast with Father. I was eating cereal, and he was trying to make himself enjoy oatmeal and failing as usual. Mother was upstairs, the sound of her jazz step class thump thump thumping through the ceiling. "Deerdra," Father said. "You should know that there are real consequences to the outcome of this mission."

"I know," I said. "I find out where the missing girl is. You take your samples from the soil and the cows. It's important, sure."

"No," he said. He paused. We could hear a chipper voice shout, "Thanks, everybody, you did it—big applause for you!" and Mother clapping and then the bathroom faucet running.

"What?" I said. Perhaps I had known all along that he was being less than honest with me, because at this moment, I had a sense that I was seeing something behind the mask, the Earth suit, the orders that had come down from the generals, and the protocols and the reports. The bathroom door opened upstairs, and Mother's steps came down the landing.

"Nothing," Father said. "It is just important that we follow protocols, submit the reports on time. "They are always watching."

"Who is always watching?" Mother said. "The NRA?"

"NSA?" I said.

"National…yes," Mother said.

"The generals. Colonel Muckinzee," Father said. "As promised, they are always watching."

Mother stared at him for a few moments and sipped at her tea. I sensed something between them, but I put it out of my mind, put the whole thing out of my mind. It was easier to focus on what was right in front of me than try to pry away layers I couldn't quite be sure were real.

Now I know that I'll have to continuing prying. Now I know that it was weakness all along to assume what I thought was true.

"Deerdra!" Father calls up the stairs, and I jump. "It is our designated meeting time," he says. "I need to brief you as Number Two."

"In a minute," I say. I text Barb, Gavin, and Kayla. I know my Earth communication device is almost certainly being monitored by the Reptilians, has been all along. For once, I think, I'll be able to turn what they think I don't know into an advantage.

We are sitting at the living room table. Father has made us both a cup of tea, and twin mugs steam next to his communication device, Mother's communication device, a small white laptop computer I have never seen before, and the metal briefcase. The laptop is open, and the briefcase is still locked. The briefcase makes a low hum that never changes. I'm not sure if my eyes are playing tricks, but I could swear that it also emits a low wattage glow, but that may just be the reflection of the overhead lights.

He notices me staring at the briefcase. "In due time," he says.

I nod. Suddenly, I feel a rise in my body temperature. My pulse quickens. Again, I'm getting conflicting results from my sympathetic nervous system: fear and anger and sadness and caring and not caring. I fight the question. It's not the time to ask. It's perhaps not the right question to ask. It's impulsive and could ruin everything, or everything that's left. But what is left?

"What?" Father says. There's kindness in his voice, and I hope again that the answer to my question is yes.

"Is it real?" I say. "Is this real?"

"This? Of course," he says. He reaches for the laptop.

"No, not this, the house and the refrigerator and whatever. I mean this." I point at him and then me, indicating, I hope, the connection between us. "Are you my father? Is she my mother? Or is this all just…just for the mission?" The tears are welling in my eyes, and my throat constricts. Stupid sympathetic nervous system.

Father places his hand on my forehead and massages it with his palm. He hasn't done this since my first day of school. We were too worried about fitting in. But it's exactly what I need—once again, I'm his little girl and only his little girl. "You are our daughter first and foremost, Deerdra," he says. "We see ourselves in you every day. We are so proud of you. Proud of everything you've accomplished. But you're more than just your mother and I. Better than us. And that's why we need to be honest with you now. I hope you can understand why we did what we did. I hope…I hope you can forgive us."

My hands turn to ice, and my heart pounds. "Father? You're scaring me."

Father closes his eyes, rubs his hands across his face, holds them briefly over his mouth. Whatever words are coming next, his subconscious is trying to keep them in.

"In the future," he says slowly, "When you think about this conversation, remember that we love you. It will seem like the least significant part of what I am about to say. You will remember everything else with such clarity, and this will seem so insignificant. Like I served you a horrible breakfast but put colored sprinkles on it. But please, Deerdra: we love you. So much."

The panic that has been dancing on the edges of my mind retreats, replaced with cold logic as the icy sensation flies away from my hands and into my heart, into my brain. Whatever comes next, I will handle it. Whatever it is will be better than all this fumbling uncertainty. "Father. I think you need to say what it is you wanted to say."

He pauses, glances around the room. He's looking for my Mother but she's not here.

"You, Deerdra, are more than *our* experiment. You are the brainchild of several rogue members of the Eighth Council of Advanced Species. At some point during the rule of the Sixth Council, the Reptilians discovered a way to adhere to the letter of our laws while ignoring the spirit. They were, through perfectly legal methods, overtaking galaxies. Obliterating whole planets using nothing but paperwork. They would overtake one or two planets with little to no sentient life. Then a third, where some beginnings of society and invention were stirring, but nothing that would qualify as truly intelligent. Like cephalopods on this planet, I suppose. Humans will pass around articles about the problem-solving abilities and rudimentary social structure of octopi in the afternoon, and then enjoy a plate of calamari for dinner."

"Soon, the Reptilians would control forty percent of a solar system, so why not let them take one more planet? Nothing has been harmed so far, and it keeps them from fighting with the other species in the Council. And one solar system sets precedent for another, and so on, and so forth."

"What does all of this have to do with me, though?" I say. "Why are you going to want me to forgive you?"

"Okay," he says. "Here goes. Some of the other—ambitious, shall we say—members of the council took note and started doing the same things. Some are vicious, darling. They'll keep the population of a planet around for food, or labor, or even sadistic entertainment. Others don't mind aligning with the vicious ones, to reap the rewards without doing the dirty work. Even some Anthean Council members. We thought there were enough species on the Council with decency and integrity, and we'd be able to keep their horrible views in check. And now with a majority on the Council."

"What does this have to do with me?" I say, louder this time.

"It was getting to be too much," he says. "You can raise a resistance against outright brutality. But how do you fight back against a slow, constant push of regulations and tort reform? It's hard enough to convince someone to send their child off to fight a war against a bloody dictator. It's impossible when the dictator wields a permit book and a handshake instead of a sword."

"And?" I say.

"And so we volunteered our child."

My emotions explode out of me, and I'm up on my feet. Not yelling, not quite, but nearly. "I'm supposed to fight a war? Against who? How? I didn't agree to any of this, and you haven't trained me to fight! My training regimen has been one session with the Triumph and 10,000 hours of movies about Earth teens!"

"We are scientists, remember. We worked on you."

"Worked? On me?"

He runs a hand through his hair and fidgets with his tie. "We gave you some…enhancements. Several members of our group—we called ourselves the Recalibrators—studied with Reptilian scientists and learned about their genetic modification techniques. We modified your DNA a bit. It's one of the reasons why we put you in that room in the center of the ship during our journey out—I didn't want to risk any cosmic radiation altering your DNA anymore. Because you are so special."

"Special?" I look at my hands, my arms. "This isn't even my real body," I say.

"Exactly! And your real body is…well, special. You're able to adapt to new environments better than anyone other than the Reptilians. Physically and mentally. You're stronger, more agile, and faster-healing. But it's your brain, who you are, everything that makes you Deerdra, that we're so excited about. You adapt, sweetheart. Think about everything you've done. You learned about an entire society through their mythology, but you were able to see that not all humans act like characters on a screen. You let them be messy and inconsistent, and you still call them friends. And that's what we need. I am sure there will be fighting, eventually, but before then, we need strong uniters who will join these groups together and convince them that there is something worth fighting for."

"That's not me," I say. I stand, walk to the corner, and look out the window. The neighbors are putting mulch around their flowers.

Father puts the metal briefcase on the table. "That is where this comes in," he says.

"And what is that?"

"This. And you? Together?" he says. A smile comes across his face, a scientist proud of his work. "The most powerful weapon in the known universe."

Chapter 45
Us against the Universe

"…and that's what I know."

We're back in Gavin's basement, surrounded by untouched chips and cookies. It looks like Gavin's mom was so delighted by our last get-together that she purchased an entire snack aisle. Nobody has an appetite right now, but my human friends continue to amaze me. I've told them that my species is, really, no better than Mrs. V and the Reptilians. Our short-term acquisition plan is friendlier—it's easier to tell them that a few of the generically good-looking celebrities and government officials they see on TV are part of my species, while those shrieking housewives are Reptilians. *They're* the ones who would drop a bomb into a volcano. *They're* the ones that would keep some humans around as an easy lunch for their hatchlings. *My* people would bring technology and good television! *My* people would encourage peace among all the species.

And my people would gradually reduce human fertility. They'd suspect something eventually, but by then, the decreased replacement rate of humans would work in our favor. Besides, isn't it better? More resources for the existing humans and their (smaller) families! Less traffic! More luxuries! But still: eventually, the humans would die off, and we'd remain. And that doesn't seem fair.

So. Gavin. Barb. Kayla. Me. Maybe the only four beings on this planet who are dedicated to saving it from the Reptilians. And from my own people.

Someday in the future, after decades on Earth, maybe humans will stop surprising me. But I'm still shocked and humbled by the reactions of my friends. They're angry, to be sure. Angry that their futures are being decided for them. Angry that if the Reptilians take over, they wouldn't have a chance to say goodbye to their families. In Kayla's case, angry that her mother has had the Reptilians on their TV almost nonstop for over a decade.

"I grew up with them just on in the background, Deerdra! A few years ago, I totally had a crush on Logan! My mom got me a #TeamLogan T-shirt, and I wore it as pajamas! What the hell, Mom? I'm supposed to trust her opinion on anything, when she's considered those vapid, murderous bitches entertainment for my entire childhood?"

Through all of it, though, my friends trust me. They trust that I'm on their side and that I've basically had an intergalactic #TeamLogan experience. I was raised thinking our mission was right and not questioning anything. But no longer. My friends and their people need a chance to grow and thrive. Maybe someday, they'll even develop faster-than-light technology and become members of the Council themselves. But for now, it's four of us against the universe.

No. Eunice Tiffany is out there somewhere. Probably in California. That makes five. And that's why we're here—we need to plan.

"Okay. I think we need a two-pronged plan of attack. We know there are Reptilian egg clutches around here: that's why Eunice and my father spent so much time exploring thc area. I can check our systems—there has to be some sort of prediction algorithm that will help us find them.

"When we find them, we need to alter the chemistry of the air around them. Change up the ratio of gasses, make them warmer or cooler than normal. Whatever it is, we need those eggs to adapt to a set of conditions that aren't true to the Earth's biome. If we smash the eggs, we smash them once. If we reprogram them with bad data, it'll screw up the next few generations of egg clutches, easy. That should buy us a few months. Hopefully, that's long enough to find Eunice. I think that means I'm headed to California. Who's staying here, and who's coming with me?"

Barb is the first to speak. Her lipstick (maroon with golden sparkles) and outfit (ripped jeans and an old sweatshirt held together with safety pins), usually part of the overall Barb Experience, seem like a costume today. In her heart, Barb is truly brave and fiercely loyal to her friends. But I can tell she's longing for an easier life right now. One where she rages against the tyranny of upper-middle-class Indiana teenagers, not lizard-like people with warp technology.

"I have to stay. I'll look for the eggs! I'll ride my bike like I'm training for the Tour de France. But Deerdra—I'm seventeen. Seventeen-year-olds don't save the world." Tears start to slip out of her eyes.

I give her a hug. "Finding those eggs is saving the world. It was stupid and dangerous for me to assume that any of you would come with me. Nobody will suspect anything if I go by myself. The homeschooled girl couldn't cut it. I can file a few things from Mother and Father and be gone in a few days. You all should stay."

Kayla wraps her arm around Barb. "You want a buddy on those bike rides? As long as you don't say anything about my green bike shorts…"

"I don't know if our species deserves to be saved if your horrible fashion choices are part of the deal." They both laugh, tears in their eyes.

"Oh, come on, Hermione," Barb says, pointing a cookie at me. "And you, Hermione." She points to Gavin. "And even you Neville Longbottom." She points at Kayla.

Kayla throws her a look but giggles, and then Gavin and I are giggling, too, and it's as if a small bit of air has been let out of the room and the atmosphere is lighter, if only for a moment.

"So, the plan," Kayla says. "I did this geospatial data analysis MOOC last summer?"

"You did what?" Gavin says.

"You think all those Instagram followers are about my good looks?" Kayla asks.

"Yes," Barb says. The two of them laugh and share a look. A private joke.

"Regardless of my fourteen thousand and growing Instagram followers," Kayla says, and Barb snorts a laugh. "Regardless of that. I also know a few things about geospatial data analysis, and I took the spreadsheets from Eunice Tiffany and your parents and ran them through some analysis, overlaid onto Google Earth, and…" She holds up her tablet, and there's a map of Indiana with several spots outlined in dark red. "I think we start here. These spots are the places where the eggs were most likely to be laid."

"Fourteen thousand Instagram followers," Barb says.

"Indeed," Kayla says.

"So that's one part," Gavin says. "Deerdra? What's the…there's another part to this, right? The Reptilians? Your parents?"

I take a moment to collect my thoughts. How to even start? But they've accepted everything else. They have accepted me for who I am, and even after knowing the danger I've put them in, they're here, eating Chips Ahoy and making new inside jokes.

"So, it turns out," I say, trying to sound casual, or jokey, or not like I'm about to cry, "that I'm kind of like a…weapon. Big weapon? Kind of like I was engineered to counterbalance the dominance of the Reptilians. Or something like that?"

"Engineered," Kayla says. "Is that normal for…Eunice never said anything about that, is what I mean. Not that she told me everything. Obviously."

"It's normal for certain things. In certain ways. Not the way it was done here. My parents are part of a group called the Recalibrators…"

"That is a terrible name," Barb says. "Were they like an eighties teen-film cover band? 'We're the Recalibrators, and this is a little song called Don't You Forget About Me…'"

"Don't you da da da da da forget about me, don't you…" Gavin sings lightly. "Yeah, that works."

"So, Recalibrators?" Kayla says, steering the conversation back to me.

"Yes. Recalibrators. They, well, before me. They were part of a group of scientists that were brought together during better times. More optimistic times. When it seemed like the Reptilians might legitimately uphold the spirit of the Council. In that spirit, my parents learned things, things about the Reptilians, how they are how they are. They used those things in me. That's why I am able to do some of the things I can do."

"So you're not Hermione after all," Barb says. She stands and comes over to me. She puts a hand on my shoulder. "You're Harry, Deerdra."

I'm embarrassed, and I feel the heat rising in my cheeks. "That's not a bad analogy as I understand it," I say. "Missing a lightning-bolt scar but other than that it's not bad."

"Scar would be kind of badass, wouldn't it?" Gavin says.

"Maybe would have been a bit of a giveaway?" Barb says.

"So the plan part of this plan then," Kayla says.

"The plan part," I say. "I'm still working on that. But I know one thing: I'm going to have to do the last part alone."

We sit there for a moment, the air filled with tension again. Everybody pokes at their food. From upstairs, a television turns on, and we hear women shouting at one another. I look to Barb, whose face is turning toward the noise. I look to Kayla. To Gavin.

"Are you kidding me?" Gavin says.

"The housewives," Kayla says. "Oh my God, I'd recognize that voice anywhere."

Barb snorts a laugh again, and then we are all laughing, giggling, struggling for air, and wiping our eyes.

"Well, that's appropriate," Barb says finally.

"How?" I say.

"You're not going alone," she says. "No way you're going alone."

"We're with you," Kayla says.

"Whatever that means," Gavin says.

PROTOCOL INITIATION REQUEST FORM:

Please use the following form for initiation of standard protocols 1 through 232. All fields are required. Please note that data will not be saved automatically: do not forget to click on the "submit" button at the bottom of this form. If you require content-editing tools, or need to save your work as you go, it is strongly recommended that you write answers out in a word processing program with save capabilities and copy your work into the form below. As you should be aware, immediate assistance cannot be requested. This form should be used for all assistance or protocol initiation requests.

Please note that this form does not guarantee protocol initiation. General Services reviews all form submissions, passes requests on to the appropriate governing body, and manages messaging. See your training materials for more information about communication processes and protocols. A response will be delivered through standard communication systems within forty-eight Earth hours of the submission of this form. If a protocol request is denied, a subsequent request will be denied, as well, and this form has been engineered to ensure that each Mission Group may initiate each protocol only once. See your training materials, page 49, chart A, for more information and a detailed explanation of the protocol request system.

PROTOCOL INITIATION:

Are you requesting a protocol initiation?
[X] Yes. [ ] No.

What type of protocol would you like to initiate today?
[X] Evacuation

Please indicate the level of Protocol Evacuation you would like to initiate today: [7]

Please indicate status notification level:
[Urgent]

PERSONAL INFORMATION:

Earth Name: William Mobilius Grey

ID Number: Terranaut 3232x-ii9

Per General Services official guidelines, this form may only be accessed by Mission Commanders. Are you the Mission Commander?

[X] Yes. [ ] No.

MISSION INFORMATION:

Location: Outpost 3429-E, Orion-Cygnus Arm

Mission ID Number: [9922xByi22]

Mission Name: Earth Reconnaissance, Sample Collection, Threat Assessment Continuation 3

Attending Colonel: [Colonel Muckinzee]

Attending General: [General Primicerius]

MISSION STAFF:

Please indicate all mission staff members, all levels.

Second-in-Command ID Number: [Terranaut 3233x-ii9]

Second-in-Command Earth Name: [Stefanie Alberius Grey]

Mission Staff 1 ID Number: [Terranaut 3231x-ii9]

Mission Staff 1 Earth Name: [Deerdra Grey]

DETAILS:

Use the fields below to provide details about the nature of your protocol initiation request. This information will be used to assess the request and formulate a strategy, should strategy formulation be required. Be brief but detailed. Be absolutely honest and transparent about all situations.

All information should be entered as single sentences.

Do not forget to hit the submit button at the bottom of the form. Your information will not automatically save. See instructions at the top of this form if you have any questions.

Please provide details about the nature of your request: why are you making this protocol initiation request?

This request is for evacuation and extraction of all mission members.

Current threat levels are extremely high.

Mission situation has escalated to an extent that Mission Success Algorithm on page 22 of orientation materials now indicates a "strongly unlikely" to meet success.

Second-in-Command has been abducted by members of Reptilia planet and is being held at an undisclosed location.

I believe the appropriate Learned Generals are currently considering a pact in which Second-in-Command is released from Reptilia planet representatives on the condition that Earth is ceded to Reptilian control.

Mission Staff 1 is experiencing extreme stress levels.

Mission Staff 1's extreme stress levels are directly related to mission goals and objectives.

Mission Staff 1's extreme stress levels are partially related to the mission's necessary physical environment of the biosuit and sympathetic nervous system and attendant emotional chemistry formulation, sixteen-year-old Earth girl.

Due to prior three notes, Mission Staff 1 is showing signs of Terranaut Dislocation Disorder, as indicated on page 78 of our orientation materials: confusion, rapid swings of emotion, distrust, rebellious tendencies, speaking out, not fitting in, disobeying orders, and general unruliness.

While I realize the following may not be considered in evaluation of this protocol initiation request, Mission Staff 1 is my daughter.

While I realize the following may not be considered in evaluation of this protocol initiation request and may also be used in evaluation of my own mission performance and especially the degree to which I succeeded or failed as a Mission Leader, it is extremely hard for me to see Mission Staff 1 in this condition.

While I realize the following may not be considered in evaluation of this protocol initiation request and may also be used in evaluation of my own mission performance and especially the degree to which I succeeded or failed as a Mission Leader, I believe I am no longer able to compartmentalize my paternal relationship with Mission Staff 1.

While I realize the following may not be considered in evaluation of this protocol initiation request and may also be used in evaluation of my own mission performance and especially the degree to which I succeeded or failed as a Mission Leader, Mission Staff 1 needs her father, and I intend to act primarily in this capacity until date of extraction.

To the extent possible, please list what you believe to be the possible ramifications of a denial of this protocol initiation request. Consider, especially, potential risks for mission success, mission team, and other threats.

As Learned Generals already know, the mission is currently in jeopardy.

It seems likely that future control of Earth will be given to Reptilia Planet representatives.

This is fine, but given this condition, I do not understand how this request would be denied by Learned Generals.

It seems likely that a denial of this request would lead to the direct or eventual cessation of existence of Mission Team.

It seems likely that Mission Team would die.

Please provide any other relevant details or information you believe General Services should know about this request.

If choices need to be made, Mission Leader requests priority extraction in the following order: Mission Staff 1, Second-in-Command, Mission Leader.

Chapter 46
I'm Ready

We park near the road as planned. I thought I would be nervous, but that's not the feeling I'm experiencing right now. If I could possibly make it another year in this environment, I might someday be able to identify the particular emotion. For right now, "ready" is the word that comes to mind.

We sit in the car. Father turns up the radio. "This old town, filled with sin, it'll swallow you in-iiiiin if you've got, the money to burn…" the singer sings. If things go poorly, I may miss this music. If things go well, I may use my personal computer device to find out who exactly sings this song.

They are at the same table, Mrs. V and the two men. There's no sign of my mother. They're all eating vanilla ice cream cones. My mother is still missing, and I'm about to defy direct orders from my father and Mission Leader, and they are licking at soft serve, staring straight ahead. Mrs. V motions from the picnic bench. She smiles, waves us toward her, and picks up her phone.

"Mother is not there," I say. "Should we…"

"It is okay," Father says. "It is probably okay."

"Nothing about this is okay," I say.

"I mean probably they have delivered your mother in another way. Another mechanism."

"Mechanism?"

"She may be back at the Earth house. Or she may be transferred."

"Transferred to?"

"It would be ships. Given the…situation. They would probably skip the middleman and take her directly to a ship in a stable galaxy, somewhere the Council has approved for temporary holding."

"The middleman being Earth," I say.

"Yes," Father says. "The Council has spoken." He says this last part as if he's talking about an immutable law of physics, and I realize it's exactly how he feels about the Council. I admire how sure he is about all of it—our place here on Earth, the Earth people, the Council, and the decision that has been handed down.

"I'm ready," I say. I put my hand on the backpack.

Father places his hand on mine. "Deerdra," he says. "I'm so sorry. I...we...we could have said no to this. We could have stayed at home. We could be..." He stops, and I know why. "I don't know where we could be," he says. "I don't know where we're going."

"No, it's okay," I say. "It really is. I'm ready for this. We need to do this. I need to do this."

He shifts in his seat, and I can see his face shift, as well, from Father to Mission Leader. "You can carry the briefcase in the backpack, and it will still work," he says. "It just has to be in contact with your biosuit, has to...know it is you, in order to work in the proper way."

"In order to wipe those doggone Reptilians off the face of the Earth."

"I do not know that I would phrase it the same way, but it will get us out of this situation and perhaps send a message."

"And you'll be?"

"Hopefully with your mother, wherever she is."

I nod. In the distance, Mrs. V waves. She stands. Father's communications device buzzes, and he checks the screen. "She says, get your pretty little fanny...fanny?"

"It means the behind, the buttocks area?"

"...get your pretty little fanny over here, and let's do this," he finishes.

I lean over and hug him. I've gotten used to the smell of his biosuit, and I breathe it in one last time—soil and mint and Speed Stick deodorant. "Okay," I say. "Let's do it to it."

"Do it, to it?" Father says.

I lift the backpack. It's heavy with the briefcase. I can feel the machinery starting up, hear it whirring softly. "It's an expression," I say. "I love you, Father."

"The protocol?" Father says. "You are invoking the protocol?"

I look at him and then realize he's joking. A small miracle in itself. "I'll see you on the other side," I say. "Wherever that is."

"I love you, too," he says. "Not protocol." He stares straight ahead.

I get out of the car.

Mrs. V points at her watch, an exaggerated gesture that I believe is intended to break the tension of the situation. Humor can work that way, but Mrs. V is no Barb, and I take the Triumph out of my pocket—smooth, the way Father taught me this afternoon—and put my fingers together.

I'm not sure what happens first, but there's a snap and a buzz, and the beam is moving from the Triumph toward the picnic table, and I'm walking fast toward them as fire erupts and half the table is gone. At the same time, they seem to levitate up and then out, moving fast, projecting themselves toward the trees. Their legs are moving, but I don't know if they're touching the ground, and then they're there, hidden in the trees, the treetops, and the picnic table is burning and I smell wood on fire and a kind of electricity I don't believe I have ever smelled before.

There are shouts from the Dairy Queen, but they register like murmurs in a high school hallway, distant and unimportant to this moment. I keep moving. The backpack was a burden and then a weight, and now it feels like an engine, a part of me, moving my legs forward, projecting flames out of the Triumph as I aim it toward the woods and press my fingers together. There's more power in this volley. I know this instinctively, but I don't know how and I don't pause to consider this increase in my strength. The shouting from the Dairy Queen continues. Somewhere in the distance, an alarm, a siren. All of this happens at a different level, like a dream, something under the surface. I press my fingers together and watch a tree disappear—whoosh zip and it is gone. One of the men in black suits is left hanging, dangling in midair. I aim the Triumph, and he moves laterally into another tree. A question flashes through my mind: would I have killed him? But my legs are moving forward, the machine pushing me toward them, toward their destruction.

A flash from the trees, and I feel a soft electric push, and a halo of energy bounces off me, regroups, bounds back toward its source, and peters out halfway to the forest. They've shot at me, and something has repelled the burst. Somehow, this makes sense, and I continue walking, the ground now grassy under my feet. The woods are yards away.

"Hey!" The familiar voice makes me pause. I have to force my legs to pause the steady churn. Pausing is all I can do.

"Hey, losers, get out here and fight like Danaville High Foxes!" No, I think. No no no.

"Hey, losers!" From the other direction now.

I force myself to stop. Another burst comes from the trees and bounces off me. This one seems to penetrate slightly deeper, and I feel an electric shock, a deep ache inside as if something has tapped the pain center in my sympathetic nervous system. I wobble and nearly fall. Turning, I see Barb to my left, Gavin and Kayla to my right. They're on the edge of the forest, hiding behind trees. They're carrying baseball bats and metal garbage-can lids as shields. I have no idea what they're thinking. I love them. I need to get them out of here.

Another blast hits me, and it's worse than the last. I'm knocked off my feet. For a moment, I feel the full weight of the backpack, pressing me to the ground like a stone. Gavin shouts and takes a step toward me. The ground near him immediately erupts into flame. He's bounced toward the trees and lands on his back. A red bloom opens up on his arm. Just as Kayla grabs him, another burst behind them.

"Over here, assholes!" Barb yells. She shouts and waves from the other side. She waves a plastic lightsaber I know she bought at Walmart last week.

Gavin. Kayla. Barb. I feel a flush of emotion, and then I'm standing again, walking toward the woods. I spin the Triumph, and a tree disappears. Then another. A flash from the tree line and I feel the energy bounce off me with a brief zip. A flash of pain and I'm moving again.

Another flash but it isn't headed to me. I look to the right. Gavin shrieks, the worst sound I've ever heard. Next to him, the ground is smoking and where Kayla used to be, there's a smoldering indentation. Gavin looks around wildly, and his gaze stops a few yards to his left. It locks on the ground. "Kayla!" he shouts. "Kayla!" He stands there, frozen.

Kayla. I flash on her smiling, sipping coffee, writing notes in Trig class, laughing with Barb in Gavin's basement. Smart and funny and beautiful and kind Kayla.

"Kayla!" I turn to see Barb running across the field. I don't think, don't worry about extending my second hand, just level the Triumph toward the woods, and a wall of flame extends toward the trees. Fire returns from the trees, and Barb is nearly hit. I intensify my attack on the tree line, focus on where I see the energy coming. Barb is nearly hit and she stumbles but keeps on going. Finally, she makes it to Gavin. She pauses and looks at the embers where Kayla used to be, and then to that spot a few yards away, then she grabs Gavin and pulls him back into the trees.

I've been firing without thinking about anything, about the plan or my intentions or whether Father has been retrieved and made it back to where they are holding Mother. Nothing. Just my friends.

"Halt fire!" Mrs. V shouts from somewhere in the trees. "Halt! Cease fire." She's breathing heavy and her voice is rough and foreign. I wonder if her biosuit is slipping, like Jerkhin, but that couldn't be. They're too advanced. "You are in violation of Council of Advanced Species Ordinance…334…Regarding Homestead Operations…on Foreign Planets Harboring Less Advanced Species!" she shouts. "By the…power…vested in me by the Council of Advanced Species, I order you to cease and desist at once and to return to the nearest retrieval area for immediate imprisonment under the terms of…"

I put my fingers together and put a blast toward where she's shouting. I'm ready for this to be over.

"Not cute!" she shouts.

I send another beam of fire toward the trees.

Sirens are getting louder. Barb and Gavin are circling back to the Dairy Queen, going the long way through the cornfield. I see police cars and fire trucks pulling into the parking lot. In the space where Kayla was standing, grey smoke trickles up toward the sky. I don't look at that other space. I can't. Not now.

"Well, now you did it," Mrs. V says. She comes out of the trees and hovers in the air. She has shed her Earth skin, and she dangles there in her true appearance, green skin glowing in the dusk, yellow eyes. She's beautiful in her own way now, not the way of the housewives. It seems immediately ridiculous that she would ever have blonde hair, those thin biceps. She floats, and energy ripples off her, and for the first time, I'm genuinely afraid.

"You are in violation of Council of Advanced Species Ordinance 334 Regarding Homestead Operation on Foreign Planets Harboring Less Advanced Species," she says. Her voice is low and thick. Reptilian.

I take another step, minding Barb and Gavin's progress through the field. The sirens are getting louder and the shouts closer.

"I don't care," I say. "I don't care what I'm in violation of, and I don't care who you represent. I. Don't. Care. Not today." I hold up the Triumph, feel the energy running through me. She shoots another blast at me, and I step past it like I'm passing through a waterfall—a quick electric zing and it's behind me. She backs up, still hovering about the trees. "Today I am stronger than you," I say. I send a beam straight at her, and she swerves to the side. "Go home," I say. "Go back. Today, this is how it ends."

"You are making a very significant mistake," she says.

"I'm seventeen years old," I say. "I have nothing but my mistakes to make, and today I am making them all." I feel energy—from the sun or the backpack or my own incandescent rage, I can't tell—course through me and into the Triumph. I aim another beam at her. But before it hits the trees, she's gone.

Chapter 47
After

The next few hours are a blur. The local police arrive right after Mrs. V disappears, but soon, a few black sedans roll in, and agents in dark suits replace the local force. We sit with Kayla, waiting for her to open her eyes and start sparring with Barb. But her eyes stay closed as we straighten her outfit, and they stay closed as the agents roll up a gurney with a long, zippered bag.

"No. Jesus, no." Barb's throat is constricted from crying, and the words shoot out like fireballs from my Triumph.

Barb runs away toward the parking lot, and Gavin trails her. I wipe tears from my face—my people don't cry, but my biosuit's reaction is the only thing that feels natural right now. "Let me help. Please. For my friend."

The assisting agent lowers the gurney, and we carefully lay Kayla onto it. I pull a few leaves out of her hair and rest her hands on her chest. She already doesn't look entirely like Kayla. Her face is starting to lose the smart smile that always lurked on the corners of her eyes and mouth.

All of my training said that she'd be my sworn enemy. I was The New Girl and she was the Lead Popular. I was ready for cutting remarks in the cafeteria. I was ready to trick her into telling me information about Eunice. I was ready for war, even if it was just in the halls of Danaville High. I wasn't ready for caring, snarky, charismatic Kayla.

And now I'm not ready to say goodbye to my friend.

But I walk away before they use that zipper down by her feet, and before they put her into the back of the low-slung car waiting at the edge of the clearing. I head back to the parking lot, back to Barb and Gavin. We huddle together and cry and talk to the agents when they approach us. They need details and statements about what just happened. They need us to say a few things into a video camera, which they'll stitch together into a news report. There was a gas explosion at the

Dairy Queen. The shockwave knocked down our friend and stopped her heart. We're so lucky to be alive.

Finally, it's just us and the few remaining agents out in the field gathering last-minute forensic information before they replicate the gas explosion.

We sit in silence on the trunk of Father's car, staring up into the midnight sky. Me-Gavin-Barb, one-two-three. But we're not evenly spaced—consciously or subconsciously, Barb left a little extra room on her end for Kayla.

"Deerdra?"

"Yeah, Gav?"

"Where are the Reptilians from?"

"You can't see from the northern hemisphere. If we were in Brazil right now, I could point in the general direction, but there are a few galaxies between there and here that block the light. I wouldn't be able to show you the individual star."

"Oh. Can you see your star from here?"

"Yeah." I could pull out my phone and show him a star chart, but I don't want to disturb this warm, dark stillness that's finally wrapped around us. "See that big line of haze that's going through the middle of the sky? That's the Milky Way. Now go all the way north, just above the horizon. There's this big cross, and one of the short arms is a little bendy? I'm from a white dwarf just above the bend."

"Hmm. New Mexico is different than I imagined. I was thinking more red sand than white dwarf."

"Yeah. It's not a bad place to be from. But I don't know if it's home anymore."

Gavin wraps his arm around my shoulder and squeezes, and my heart squeezes inside my chest.

I think I love Gavin. I don't know if it's friend-love or family-love or romantic-love. It's different than what I feel for Mother and Father, and eventually, I'll have to figure out what that means. But tonight, I just close my eyes and lean in.

"Well, home is where the eight-chambered heart is," Barb says. "Or whatever. You know, we know shockingly little about this whole thing where you are a being from another planet. We basically binge-watched a decade of *Star Trek* and *Ancient Aliens* here in the DQ parking lot, but I don't even know if I should be feeding you Reese's Pieces or hot sauce or human flesh."

She makes a spooky voice and waggles her fingers at me on that last one. Gavin rolls his eyes and drops his head over his shoulder at Barb. "Really?"

"Look, if I'm going to write that essay, I'm going to know the details. This thing has to get me into Harvard or Yale or at least into the good parts of Area 51. I'm going places, Gav."

"Really?"

She half nudges, half cuddles him with her side. "Deerdra could tell us the secrets of warp technology, and we could tell her about the time we took a class field trip to Little Caesars and learned the secrets of the kitchen. For the good of both our people! It would be a peacekeeping effort! We need to take some time and play twenty questions."

From a few parking spaces away, someone else chimes in. "I may be able to help with that."

The three of us look over as the owner of this new voice steps into the yellow flicker of the streetlight. I'm safely within the safe zone between rejuvenations, but the backpack must have sapped my strength. I'm hallucinating. There's no way she should be behind the secure perimeter.

"Hi, honey. Barbara, Gavin, you kids doing okay? You've had quite the night. Can I buy you an ice cream?"

"Mrs. Queen? What are you doing here? Um…the Dairy Queen closed hours ago."

"With my connections, we can get you a cone if you need a cone."

I brace myself for the swarm of agents that must be coming next. I hope they don't hurt her.

"I bet there are a lot of Danaville grads that work here, huh, Mrs. Queen," says Gavin. Bless him, he's trying to cover. Trying to get her out safely.

"I'm sure there are, but I was referring to Agent Martinez. The one in charge out there? With the glasses? If he can't pick the lock on that door, we'd kick him down to a desk in Human Resources."

"Oh. Oooookay…"

"Honey, stop worrying. I've been keeping an eye on homeschooled students from New Mexico since the days of Close Encounters. And when the old woman in charge wants an ice cream, stop making her feel guilty about it and join her. In fact, let's make it a banana split. We have a lot of plans to make. Deerdra, have you learned how to drive?"

"I can operate a vehicle, but I'm not officially licensed.. The Colonel thought it would be more authentic if I learned while I was here. And I think he was excited to see the report. 'One of the major signifiers of the transition from juvenile to adulthood,' he called it."

Mrs. Queen sniffs and raises an eyebrow. I wonder if she developed these exaggerated microexpressions in her career working with other terranauts, or if the terranauts took to her because she's easy to read when she chooses to be. "The Colonel does love his movies. So much neater than field work. And of course, he never realized your full potential. Classic upper management oversight, I'm afraid. You and I need to talk about what those field reports are going to say in the future. Tim. Tim! Be a dear and open that door for me."

Agent Martinez does as requested, and Father tags along. Soon, we're inside the restaurant, obeying Mrs. Queen's orders to draw the blinds and push tables together and, of course, make ourselves some ice cream. Extra sprinkles.

Martinez sets the table for six. Barb almost sits, then her eyes get shiny, and she pulls a seventh chair next to her. Father immediately follows suit, and I do, too. Kayla, Mother, and Jerkhin should be here. For tonight, we'll pretend they're just behind the corner, making sundaes for themselves.

Mrs. Queen reaches across the space and squeezes Barb's hand. They're wearing nearly identical nail polish. Masters of disguise think alike, I suppose. "You kids have done amazing work so far against those doggone Reptilians. Now, how do you feel about a little road trip?"

She turns over a few placemats and starts sketching.

REQUEST FOR PERSONAL LEAVE

From: Terranaut 6.54.C, Outpost 3429-E, Orion-Cygnus Arm
To: Colonel Muckinzee, Outpost NGC-6946, Fireworks Galaxy

OVERVIEW:

As I'm sure you know, I was involved in the Battle of Bovine, roughly three Earth weeks ago. My primary information source in the Eunice Tiffany case was killed in battle. Due to the overwhelming emotional and physical stress of this battle, I violated several ordinances regarding homestead operation on foreign planets harboring less advanced species.

My Second-in-Command remains abducted by the Reptilians. My Mission Leader is currently working on a side project with T.L. Martinez of the NSA.

As such, I am formally requesting personal leave from my mission. I plan to explore my current continent. I will report back with relevant agricultural and climatological data as I have time.

My return date to this mission is currently unknown. I trust my role in this mission was nonessential, and resources should be focused on returning my Second-in-Command from the Reptilians.

After all, General: I'm just a kid.

Chapter 48
On the Road

[FATHER]

Do you have everything that TLM and 👑 gave you?

YES. You and I went over the checklist five times last night.
Nice emoji, btw.

Forgive me, but I have never operated a mission without official protocol.
And thank you! They are quite humorous. 🐦💪🌀🐙🔬🏄🗿⛰👽👽👽

Look at you! I am arrogant of you!

You are PROUD of me. 😱
Be careful, Deerdra.
Stay with your friends.
Use what's in the trunk if you need to.

I always am.
You know if Barb sees this, she's opening the briefcase immediately.

Then only show this to Gavin.

Hahaha

Be safe. I love you. No protocol involved.

I love you too, Dad. Let me know if you hear anything about Mom.

<3

<3

I put my phone on the seat next to my backpack—the same pack I used on my first day of school, but I've added a few decorations. I'd like to find a new button or patch for every major stop we make on this trip—I saw that in a movie once, and it stuck out. Once we reach California, I hope it'll be full of patches and entirely unlike anything you could find in a back-to-school ad. Unique.

Mrs. Queen even asked the new janitor to solder a pin backing onto one of Kayla's old necklaces. She gave it to me on our last day of school, along with some maps and supplies and the car. The car has a rejuvenation system for me, and "some extras" that we are supposed to test once we get into some of the more remote areas of the country.

Officially, I'm going back to homeschool, Gavin is taking advantage of his advanced placement credits and enrolling in college early to get away from his troubled home, and Barb is taking a semester off to grieve. Judging by how quiet she's been for these last few weeks, it'll be good for her.

Unofficially? I touch my gold K pin and then pull out the postcard with the name of a bookstore and a smiley face.

Gavin is driving, and Barb's riding shotgun, unwrapping snacks and keeping an eye on the maps. For now, I'm in charge of playlists. Since my last big trip spanned 600 light years, I can probably keep us in music for 2,000 miles or so.

My name is Deerdra Grey. I am seventeen years old. My friends and I are going to find Eunice Tiffany and save our worlds.

THE END

Acknowledgments

From Becky and Dave: Thanks to everybody at Pandamoon for your attention, care, smarts, and time in seeing this book from a rough manuscript through a global pandemic and now out into the world as a finished product. Thanks to Zara Kramer for seeing something in our weirdo alien girl, and to Rachel Schoenbauer, Kathy Bosman, and Forrest Driskel for the smart and careful edits that made this a much better book. Thanks to Don Moore Kramer and to Pawee Dimla for taking our pretty specific vision for the cover and bringing to life what we could hardly explain in words. Thanks to all of Pandamoon for creating such a fun, productive atmosphere and making a space in the publishing world for alien girls and Real Housewives that are really Reptilians.

Thanks to our Barrelhouse family and friends for creating a community where a couple of project managers can say "we're co-writing a YA book about an alien teenage spy" and only hear support: Christina Beasley, Dan Brady, Tara Campbell, Killian Czuba, Erin Fitzgerald, Chris Gonzalez, Mike Ingram, Joe Killiany, Tom McAllister, Susan Muaddi-Darraj, Matt Perez, and Sheila Squillante, and the rest of our Barrelfamily and Barrelfriends. The best weirdos.

Special thanks to Gene Hackman and the MNPPTMC. All our love to Pizza Tom.

From Becky: Thank you, Dave, for introducing me to the Barrelhouse crew, Peruvian chicken, and The Last Waltz. And for turning a lunchtime conversation about your book idea into this fun thing that kept us connected over seven years and a thousand miles. You're the best.

To my family - Duane and Beth Syens, Amy and Troy Moore, and Sam and Sophia - I love you with all my heart. And to Bob and Jeanne Barnard, Ann and Bryan and Ray Birnschein - thank you for making me a part of your family.

Most of all, thanks to Andrew. I've spent more than half of my life studying, traveling, dog-walking, snow-shoveling, binge-watching, and even quarantining with you, and you always keep it interesting and always, always make me laugh. I love you.

From Dave: Thanks to my family for all your support of this weird thing I do! That's Don Housley, Grace Housley, Debbie Cooper, Joe Cooper, Nick Cooper, Pete Cooper, Kate Curran, Mark Liddington, Lisa Liddington, Nina Liddington, Rhea Liddington, Skip Wieder, and Linda Wieder. Thanks to my partner Lori Wieder and son Ben Housley. Your love and support mean everything to me.

Thank you, Becky! This thing never becomes anything without you and your same-brain and badass lovely writing and actually knowing that, as you once said when we decided to actually try this, "every teenage girl feels like an alien." You're the best.

About the Authors

Becky Barnard is a book nerd and a web nerd who fell in with a crew of fantastic writers and ended up writing a book with one of them. A former scientifically typical Midwestern teenager, she's now an editor at Barrelhouse and a web project manager in State College, Pennsylvania, where she lives with her husband and their awesome dog. *The Greys* is her first novel.

The Greys is Dave Housley's fourth novel. Third and a half? He wrote about half of this book, and also some other novels, and four collections of short stories. He is one of the editors and all-around do-stuff people at Barrelhouse. He is the Director of Web Strategy for Penn State Outreach and Online Education, and he lives in State College, Pennsylvania with his wife and son, two pit bulls, and a bossy cat. He tweets at @housleydave.

Your purchase of *The Greys* supports our growing community of talented authors. If you enjoyed this book, please let the author know by posting a review at https://www.pandamoonpub.com and register today to receive advance notice of new book releases, special bundles, and discounts.

Growing good ideas into great reads…one book at a time.

Visit http://www.pandamoonpublishing.com to learn about other works by our talented authors.

Mystery/Thriller/Suspense

- ***A Flash of Red*** **by Sarah K. Stephens**
- **A Rocky Series of Mysteries Book 1: *A Rocky Divorce* by Matt Coleman**
- **Ballpark Mysteries Book 1: *Murder at First Pitch* by Nicole Asselin**
- **Ballpark Mysteries Book 2: *Concession Stand Crimes* by Nicole Asselin**
- **Bodie Anderson Series Book 1: *Code Gray* by Benny Sims**
- **Crescent City Series Book 1: *Crescent City Moon* by Nola Nash**
- **Crescent City Series Book 2: *Crescent City Sin* by Nola Nash**
- **David Knight Thrillers Book 1: *The Amsterdam Deception* by Tony Ollivier**
- **Dee Rommel Mysteries Book 1: *10 DAYS* by Jule Selbo**
- **Evening in the Yellow Wood Series Book 1: *Evening in the Yellow Wood* by Laura Kemp**
- **Evening in the Yellow Wood Series Book 2: *Snow in Summer by Laura Kemp***
- ***Fate's Past*** **by Jason Huebinger**
- ***Graffiti Creek*** **by Matt Coleman**
- ***Juggling Kittens*** **by Matt Coleman**
- ***Killer Secrets*** **by Sherrie Orvik**
- ***Knights of the Shield*** **by Jeff Messick**
- ***Kricket*** **by Penni Jones**
- ***Looking into the Sun*** **by Todd Tavolazzi**
- ***On the Bricks*** **by Penni Jones**
- ***Project 137*** **by Seth Augenstein**
- ***Rogue Alliance*** **by Michelle Bellon**
- ***Sinai Unhinged*** **by Joanna Evans**
- ***Southbound*** **by Jason Beem**
- ***Suicide Souls by Penni Jones***
- ***The Juliet*** **by Laura Ellen Scott**
- ***The Last Detective*** **by Brian Cohn**
- **The Moses Winter Mysteries Book 1: *Made Safe* by Francis Sparks**

- The New Royal Mysteries Book 1: *The Mean Bone in Her Body* by Laura Ellen Scott
- The New Royal Mysteries Book 2: *Crybaby Lane* by Laura Ellen Scott
- The New Royal Mysteries Book 3: *Blue Billy* by Laura Ellen Scott
- *The Ramadan Drummer* by Randolph Splitter
- The Teratologist Series Book 1: *The Teratologist* by Ward Parker
- *The Unraveling of Brendan Meeks* by Brian Cohn
- The Zeke Adams Series Book 1: *Pariah* by Ward Parker
- The Zeke Adams Series Book 2: *Fur* by Ward Parker
- *This Darkness Got to Give* by Dave Housley
- *To Kill a Unicorn by DC Palter*

Science Fiction/Fantasy

- *Beacons* by Katie Masters
- Children of Colonodona Book 1: *The Wizard's Apprentice* by Alisse Lee Goldenberg
- Children of Colonodona Book 2: *The Island of Mystics* by Alisse Lee Goldenberg
- Dybbuk Scrolls Trilogy Book 1: *The Song of Hadariah* by Alisse Lee Goldenberg
- Dybbuk Scrolls Trilogy Book 2: *The Song of Vengeance* by Alisse Lee Goldenberg
- Dybbuk Scrolls Trilogy Book 3: *The Song of War* by Alisse Lee Goldenberg
- Everly Series Book 1: *Everly* by Meg Bonney
- Everly Series Book 2: *Rosewood Burning* by Meg Bonney
- Finder Series Book 1: *Chimera Catalyst* by Susan Kuchinskas
- Finder Series Book 2: *Singularity Syndrome* by Susan Kuchinskas
- Fried Windows Series Book 1: *Fried Windows (In a Light White Sauce)* by Elgon Williams
- Fried Windows Series Book 2: *Ninja Bread Castles* by Elgon Williams
- *Humanity Devolved* by Greyson Ferguson
- Magehunter Saga Book 1: *Magehunter* by Jeff Messick
- Magehunter Saga Book 1: *Priesthunter* by Jeff Messick
- *The Bath Salts Journals Volume One* by Alisse Lee Goldenberg and An Tran
- The Crimson Chronicles Book 1: *Crimson Forest* by Christine Gabriel
- The Crimson Chronicles Book 2: *Crimson Moon* by Christine Gabriel
- *The Greys* by Dave Housley and Becky Barnard
- The Phaethon Series Book 1: *Phaethon* by Rachel Sharp
- The Phaethon Series Book 2: *Pharos* by Rachel Sharp
- The Sitnalta Series Book 1: *Sitnalta* by Alisse Lee Goldenberg
- The Sitnalta Series Book 2: *The Kingdom Thief* by Alisse Lee Goldenberg
- The Sitnalta Series Book 3: *The City of Arches* by Alisse Lee Goldenberg
- The Sitnalta Series Book 4: *The Hedgewitch's Charm* by Alisse Lee Goldenberg

- The Sitnalta Series Book 5: *The False Princess* by Alisse Lee Goldenberg
- The Thuperman Trilogy Book 1: *Becoming Thuperman* by Elgon Williams
- The Thuperman Trilogy Book 2: *Homer Underby* by Elgon Williams
- The Thuperman Trilogy Book 3: *Thuperheros* by Elgon Williams
- The Wolfcat Chronicles Book 1: *Dammerwald by* Elgon Williams

Women's Fiction

- *Beautiful Secret* by Dana Faletti
- *Find Me in Florence* by Jule Selbo
- *The Long Way Home* by Regina West
- The Mason Siblings Series Book 1: *Love's Misadventure* by Cheri Champagne
- The Mason Siblings Series Book 2: *The Trouble with Love* by Cheri Champagne
- The Mason Siblings Series Book 3: *Love and Deceit* by Cheri Champagne
- The Mason Siblings Series Book 4: *Final Battle for Love* by Cheri Champagne
- *The Shape of the Atmosphere* by Jessica Dainty
- The To-Hell-And-Back Club Book 1: *The To-Hell-And-Back Club* by Jill Hannah Anderson
- The To-Hell-And-Back Club Book 2: *Crazy Little Town Called Love* by Jill Hannah Anderson

Non-Fiction

- *Marketing for Freelance Writers* by Robyn Roste
- *The Writer's Zen* by Jessica Reino

Made in United States
North Haven, CT
04 May 2022

18906399R00104